He kissed h

It was the surest
up fast. His mou
and what began
an immediate problem quickly became
something else entirely.

Her mouth beneath his was pliant, soft,
tempting. At first, she tried to pull free,
but Santos gave her no room to back away.
Every cell in his body demanded that he
hold her closer, tighter. He felt the pull of
her and knew that there was more at work
here than simple need. Simple attraction
for a beautiful woman.

He *had* to taste her. Had to have more
of her. Somthing stirred within, hungry,
demanding, urging him to claim her. To
take her.

Dear Reader,

Writing for the Intrigue Nocturne line is just a magical experience. Being able to turn your imagination loose and explore all of the worlds your daydreams continually visit is a treat for a writer.

In *Nevermore* you'll meet Santos, an Immortal Guardian, who was once the lover of Queen Isabella of Spain. For those of you who read my first Nocturne story, *Eternally*, you'll remember Santos and, hopefully, be glad to see him with his own book.

Of course, nothing goes smoothly for an Immortal whose duty it is to protect humanity from the demon worlds populating dimensions sometimes far too close to our own.

And when Santos meets Erin Brady, a psychic running from the demon who has promised to kill her on her birthday, nothing will ever be the same again.

Maureen

Nevermore
MAUREEN CHILD

MILLS & BOON®
Pure reading pleasure™

*First published in Great Britain 2009
by Harlequin Mills & Boon Limited,
Eton House, 18-24 Paradise Road, Richmond, Surrey TW9 1SR*

© Maureen Child 2007

ISBN: 978 0 263 87263 7

46-0109

*Harlequin Mills & Boon policy is to use papers that are
natural, renewable and recyclable products and made from
wood grown in sustainable forests. The logging and
manufacturing processes conform to the legal environmental
regulations of the country of origin.*

*Printed and bound in Spain
by Litografia Rosés S.A., Barcelona*

ABOUT THE AUTHOR

Maureen Child is a California native who loves to travel. She and her husband take off for research trips every chance they get. The author of more than sixty books, Maureen loves a happy ending and still swears that she has the best job in the world. She lives in Southern California with her husband, two children and a golden retriever with delusions of grandeur.

To Diana Ventimiglia, Thanks Diana, for keeping me on my toes and never forgetting when everything is due!

Chapter 1

Her stalker was back.

Heart pounding, breath strangling in her chest, Erin Brady darted through the crowd of tourists on the wharf in Shadow Cove, Maine.

She felt him.

"Where?" she whispered through clenched teeth, her gaze sweeping the blur of faces as she ran. It could be anyone. The teenager leaning against the fence. The old man squinting into the sun. The harried housewife trying to corral a small child.

"God, where do I go?" she muttered, not expecting an answer. All she could do was run.

The air was cold with the bite of fall. The sun was setting, spreading sheets of gold and crimson across the surface of the ocean that stretched out behind her and lapped eagerly at the pylons below the boardwalk. The sun-faded boards beneath her feet groaned and creaked with the ocean's movement, and sounded like ghosts, keening a warning.

No warning necessary, Erin thought wildly, the heels of her boots clacking against the wood planks as she ran. She *knew* she was being followed. Again. She felt the power of someone's stare burrowing into her back even as she bolted for the safety she knew she wouldn't find.

A fisherman eased back on his pole and took a step backward that had Erin clipping into his shoulder as she ran. He shouted after her, but she could only lift one hand in apology and yell, "I'm sorry. Sorry." No time. No time to be polite. No time to worry about pissing off the locals. No time for anything but finding somewhere to hide. To get out of sight.

The bucolic fishing village was packed with tourists there to see the autumn foliage. Quaintly decorated shop fronts strived to look as they might have two hundred years ago. Cobblestones paved the main street and every door was propped open, the better to induce spontaneous shopping.

Erin had been in town for a week, looking for a place to escape the crowded, suddenly terrifying streets of New York. Raised in California, she'd lived in Manhattan for years. Erin was more at home with the big-city vibe, but over the last few weeks things had changed.

Let's face it, she thought, things had changed five years ago. On her twenty-fifth birthday, she'd received a letter from the birth mother she'd never known, warning Erin that on her thirtieth birthday, her biological father was going to find her, steal her psychic abilities and then kill her.

Now, with only three weeks left before she turned the big three-O, life was getting scary. Especially since the day *someone* had shoved her off a curb in Brooklyn and into the path of an oncoming bus. Erin had survived that, thanks to a quick-moving good Samaritan. But since that day, she'd felt eyes watching her. Following her every movement.

She'd thought she would be safe tucked away in a tiny village just a half hour from the Canadian border.

Clearly, she had been wrong.

She slapped her right hand onto a light post and

used it to swing herself around the corner in her blind run. The instant her hand touched the cold, black metal though, her mind filled with the images of everyone who had touched it before her.

Visions raced through her mind so quickly, she could barely separate one from the other. *Old men, young women, boys carving their initials into the black paint, drunks leaning into the pole, a young couple nestled against it, lips locked in a hungry kiss*—she saw them all in a rapid progression despite trying to close them all out.

Not now, she thought wildly, doing her best to close down the psychic images flooding her mind. Normally, she could deal with the burst of visions erupting in her mind at the simplest touch of an object. She'd learned to pause, let the pictures rise up and fade away in their own time. Today, she couldn't afford to be distracted. Not even for an instant.

She shook her head, stumbled, waved her arms to steady herself and then raced down the cobblestone street. Erin darted in and out of the crowds as she passed one shop after another. Which one? Where should she go? Where would she be safe?

Then one shop seemed to stand out from all the others. Soft blue paint, gray shutters and a gleaming front window with gold-leaf paint proclaiming *The Ancient Sea*. Her boots slid, then grabbed the cobblestones as she ducked inside. Her instincts had prompted her to choose this shop above all the others and she was in no shape to argue with them. Besides, all that mattered was that she get off the street, out of sight, before whoever had been watching her on the wharf could find her again.

A bell over the door pealed as she stepped on the welcome mat and the old woman behind the counter gave her a blank stare and a brief nod of greeting. Erin couldn't blame the woman for not being delighted to see her. She must look half crazed. God knew that's how she felt. Breathless, terrified, lost.

Where the hell could she go?

What was she supposed to do?

"Welcome," the woman said, but the single word didn't hold much warmth. "If I can help you find something, please ask."

Sure, Erin thought frantically, tossing one glance over her shoulder at the wide window overlooking the street, *help me find the reason someone's suddenly out to get me.*

Swallowing hard, she wandered blindly down the cluttered aisle and let her gaze slide over the shelves and display cases of antiques. There was a nautical theme to every item in the store—hence, she thought, the name of the shop. Careful not to touch anything, lest she plunge herself into another series of psychic visions, Erin wandered to the back of the store, keeping her head down and her shoulders slumped in a vain attempt to disappear.

Normally, she tended to avoid antique shops. With her kind of "gift," antiques were overwhelming. Too many memories. Too many energy imprints left behind by sometimes generations of previous owners. But today, for some reason, she'd chosen this store out of all the others to hide in.

The air in the shop smelled of lavender and chicken soup. An odd combination, but somehow comforting. Steadying her heartbeat took a minute or two of concentration, but she forced herself to breathe deeply, slowly. Panic, her closest companion these days, crouched in the pit of her stomach and snarled, but Erin wouldn't give into it. Wouldn't fall apart. Not here. Not now. She couldn't afford to. She had to think. Had to figure out a way to handle the sudden upheaval that had become her life.

Only three weeks ago, she'd been the head chef in DelVeccio's, a small, but trendy restaurant in the Village. She'd built her reputation on creativity and excellence and the restaurant was just beginning to get noticed. Then one day, it all went to hell.

The bell over the shop door rang again and Erin stopped dead, half-hidden behind a display case filled with scrimshaw carvings and colorful glass balls that had once festooned fishing nets. She peeked around the edge of a bust of the Ancient Mariner, carved from driftwood and polished to a high gleam and released a breath when she saw two elderly women, chattering brightly, enter the shop.

Okay, whoever was following her, she was pretty sure it wasn't those two. No way could they have kept up with her. Not the way she'd been sprinting down Main Street. Since no one else came into the shop after the women, maybe she'd lost her stalker.

But if she had, it wouldn't be for long. Not in a town this size. "Idiot," Erin muttered, turning to the far shelf at the back of the store. "If you couldn't stay lost in Manhattan, what made you think you could do it here?"

"I beg your pardon," the shopkeeper asked, appearing beside her, "were you speaking to me?"

"No, sorry," Erin said and forced a smile she was fairly sure looked as ghastly as she felt. "Just thinking out loud."

"I see." The woman, in her seventies, was dressed in a long, flowing red caftan over black slacks and her snow-white hair was done up in an elaborate French twist at the back of her head. Her blue eyes studied Erin for a long moment, then she asked, "I noticed you were looking at the scrimshaw. Is there something I can show you?"

"Um, no, thanks. I'm really just browsing." And hiding from whoever was outside that door. It probably wasn't safe to stay in one place too long, either, but she couldn't seem to make herself walk through that front door. She *had* to stay here. But for how long?

"Fine. But please be careful around the antiquities," she said and quietly moved away to offer assistance to the two elderly women arguing over a teak tea chest.

Erin sighed and glanced around at the shelves

full of merchandise. She wondered if the woman would mind if she just stayed here in the shop, hidden away for a month or two. But as soon as she thought it, Erin knew hiding wasn't the answer. Whoever was following her would find her again. And if she stayed in this shop, she'd be trapped.

But wasn't she trapped already? She hadn't been safe at home and running hadn't helped the situation any. What she needed were some answers. Answers that made sense. Answers about the birth mother who'd reached out from who knew where to set into motion dangers Erin had no idea how to fight.

She stepped away from the wide front window and moved deeper into the shadows toward the back of the shop. Up near the cash register, the three women were chattering, their voices a steady stream of noise that both comforted and annoyed.

Moving beyond the reach of sunlight, Erin stepped into the shadowy corner where the less impressive antiques were shelved haphazardly. Cracking leather tobacco pouches were crowded alongside mortar and pestles. Wooden cups and bowls were stacked in uneven towers and a pewter platter lay gleaming dully in the dim, overhead light.

There was nothing there to intrigue anyone.
Nothing to dazzle the imagination or fire curiosity. And yet, Erin was drawn to the back shelf,
her gaze landing on the butt end of a lone ivory
knife, partially hidden behind the platter. Her
fingers itched to touch the knife even while her
mind pulled back from the thought. One touch
and she knew she would see the memories locked
into that weapon. She would see the person who
had held it, used it, worn it on his hip.

And yet…she moved in closer, holding her
breath as her gaze locked on that knife. There was
something about it. Something that called to her.

The ivory handle of the knife was intricately
carved, though its edges were worn with time.
Erin leaned in, heart racing. She picked out the
designs in the yellowed ivory and recognized them
as dolphins cresting the tops of waves.

"A seaman, then," she whispered, her voice
hardly more than a breath. The edges of the knife
seemed to glow as she watched it, as if it had been
lying here in the shadows of this shop forever,
just waiting for her to arrive and find it.

That thought brought her up short for a second
or two. Was *this* the reason she'd chosen this particular shop to hide in? Was her psychometry

getting stronger? Was she developing deeper psychic abilities? Was it just another piece of the puzzle surrounding the last few weeks?

"Oh, God. I don't know how much more of this I can take, you know?" She could deal with the "touch and see" *gift* she already had. But she so didn't want any extra psychic prizes. Still, she couldn't ignore the urge to touch that knife. Whether it was fate she'd landed in this store or pure chance, that knife meant *something*. So, she took another shaky breath and closed her hand around the ivory handle, pulling it from the darkness into the light.

The cool, carved bone warmed in her hand. Erin tightened her grip, pulled in a deep breath of air and held it, trying to prepare for what was to come. But nothing could have prepared her.

Instantly, Erin's world shifted, shattered and rebuilt itself again. She was used to this, having experienced these vivid visions all of her life. But this time, she thought, as she felt the wind in her hair and the sea spray on her face, it was *different*.

More vivid.

More immediate.

The cluttered antique shop dissolved into mist and Erin gasped as she tumbled into her vision.

Men shouted all around her, their voices clamoring to be heard over the roar of the wind and the crash of the waves pounding against the wooden hull of the ship she rode.

The moonless night seemed as black as the inside of a bag. Yet, there were pinpoints of light, too. Lanterns, flying crazily in the wind, tossing shadows across the boat and the faces of the men who worked frantically to save the ship from the storm.

She turned in a slow circle, a part of the scene and yet separate from it. On either side of the sailing ship, another ship fought the same raging storm and the shouts of their crews floated like phantoms on the wind. Erin experienced a wild surge of emotion as the fear from the past filled her. Rationally, she knew that this world and all the men now screaming and fighting the storm for their very survival had faded into the mists of time centuries before.

But now, Erin stood on the heaving deck of the ship and was bathed in icy sea spray. Caught in the memories trapped within the ivory-handled knife, she felt the wind tearing at her hair with cold, tenacious fingers. She experienced the twist of terror gripping the long-dead men.

Helplessness choked her as she was forced to

admit once again that there was nothing she could do to alter the vision flooding her. No way she could help these men, ease their fears. Inhaling deeply, she tipped her head back to see men climbing the rigging, hurrying to furl the sails before they could be shredded. She watched others slide and skid across the wet deck, screaming for help and shouting to God.

Then *he* stepped into her line of vision. Tall, with shoulders broad enough to land an airplane on, he wore brown leather pants, a long-sleeved white shirt and knee-high black boots. His dark brown hair was tied at the nape of his neck and hung to the middle of his back. His dark eyes swept the deck and he shouted orders as he moved with sure steps toward the railing. He leaned into the wind, squinting into the fury of the storm, as if trying to gauge the danger they faced.

There was no fear in his expression, just a nerveless acceptance. She didn't need to see the ivory-handled knife strapped to his hip to know that he was the owner of the knife she still held with a grip that made her fingers ache. Yet there it was, gleaming new and bright in the darkness. Existing both in the past and the present where Erin stood in an antique store in Maine.

"*¡Manolo,*" he shouted into the wind, grabbed a length of rope off the railing and glared at a smaller man sliding across the deck, "*venido aquí!*"

The man rushed toward him.

"*Lleve la cuerda el arco de la nave.*"

"*Sí, sí, Señor Santos,*" the short man shouted, then took the rope from Santos and ran with it down the length of the ship.

Santos. His name was Santos, Erin thought, completely caught up in the man and his world as they all fought together to stave off death. His energy was so strongly imprinted on the knife, it was as if it was charged with his very soul, giving her a clearer glimpse of the past than she'd ever experienced before.

Erin wished suddenly that she could speak Spanish. That she could understand what everyone—okay, mostly Santos—was saying. But as her vision swirled around her and the men on the boats dropped to their knees to pray to a God who clearly wasn't listening, she knew it wouldn't matter. Whatever Santos had been—his time was gone.

And knowing that this really amazing-looking man was no more than a memory tore at Erin in a way she hadn't expected. She felt as though she should be mourning him—though he stood not a foot away from her, alive and strong and magnificent.

He turned then and seemed to look right at her. His dark eyes flickered with shock and he took a step toward her. *"¿Qué?"*

"No," Erin whispered and swallowed hard. "That's impossible. You can't see me. The visions only work one way."

"¿Cuales son usted?" he asked, still staring at her as though she'd dropped from heaven and she supposed that's what it must have looked like to him.

But how could it look like anything to him? How was he seeing her? How was a connection bridged through the centuries? And what the hell was he saying to her?

"This can't be happening," she said and took a step back, shaking her head as though the action alone would convince her that none of this was taking place.

"¿Cómo usted consiguió aquí?" he demanded and the strength of his voice carried over the fury of the storm. He was a man used to giving orders and seeing them obeyed.

She couldn't give him what he wanted. She had

no idea what he was saying. And just for a moment, Erin felt a punch of disappointment and grief so fierce, it shook her to her soul.

He was real. Alive. More alive than any other vision she'd known. And yet, in her time, his bones had gone to dust long before she was even born, and that knowledge filled her with a sense of emptiness that threatened to swallow her as surely as the ocean was trying to swallow the ship of the past.

"You really can see me."

His dark eyes narrowed on her. *"¿Está usted un ángel?"*

God, why hadn't she taken Spanish instead of French in high school?

The ship bucked and rolled with a wave that crashed into the side of the hull, sending icy cold water spraying over the deck. *"¿Qué usted desean?"*

Weird. And shocking.

Almost as shocking as seeing another man come up behind him and pull the bone-handled knife from Santos's belt.

"Santos, look out!" She shouted it, but it was already too late.

Distracted, he had no time to prevent the other

man from stabbing the bone-handled knife up and into his back. Santos howled in fury and pain— glaring at Erin as if this were all her fault.

She could do nothing for him, even as the attacker, clutching the bloodied knife, backed away, shouting, *"¡Para el honor de mi reina!"*

Erin reached for Santos, though she knew it was useless and while she stood, a helpless observer, locked in the past, a rogue wave swept up over the side of the ship, plucked Santos from the deck and dragged him down beneath the surface of the black, churning water.

Erin dragged air into her lungs and fought the threat of tears that shuddered through her along with a profound sense of loss.

But before she could drop the knife, another vision erupted in her mind, sending her on a roller-coaster ride of blurred colors, blaring sounds and jolting emotions.

Santos again. His hair was shorter, though still clubbed at the back of his neck, his ponytail only reaching his shoulders now. He wore black pants, scuffed black boots and a long black coat that spun around his long legs as he moved with the grace of a stalking panther.

She stared hard at the scene unfolding before

her as the man she'd watch die moments ago fought an opponent like a master swordsman. His long blade slashing at a smaller, quicker man with flames in his eyes, Santos laughed, throwing his head back, enjoying this fight, thrilling to the challenge, the danger.

She felt his joy in the battle, and his complete confidence in his abilities and wanted to laugh with him. But what was happening? What were her visions showing her? They'd never been this disjointed before. Never showed her a man dying only to show him alive and well and…she looked around and caught sight of a small green and white sign…in San Diego?

Erin stood on a modern city street and tried to make sense of what she was seeing. It couldn't be true. He'd died centuries before. Yet here he was now, in this time. Her time. Healthy. Alive.

His dark eyes were the same. His features were harsher, sterner, but still, it was him. The man she'd seen on the sailing ship. The man who had reached across a chasm of centuries to connect with her at the moment of his death.

The man she'd seen stabbed and drowned.

"Another day, Guardian!" The small man screamed in rage, and then the sword fight ended in a blurring shift of color and light and then Santos was alone under the hazy yellow glow of a streetlamp.

"Cowardly demon," Santos muttered, sliding his sword into the scabbard he wore beneath his long black coat. "Shifting to escape a battle. Does no one have honor anymore?"

"Demon?" Erin whispered, wondering what the hell he was talking about.

Santos whirled around, instinctively pulling a knife from his belt and dropping into a crouch as his long black coat swirled out around him. He scowled, narrowed his gaze and stared directly into Erin's eyes, as he had before during the storm on the ship.

Impossible, but again he seemed to be staring right at her.

"You?" This time, he spoke English. Rising slowly, he kept his knife at his side in a tight fist and took a step toward her. "Who the hell are you? Where did you come from?"

"This can't be happening," Erin whispered.

Instantly, she dropped the bone-handled knife, effectively ending the vision, and a heartbeat later she found herself back in the antique store in Maine. She was stretched out on the cold tile floor, staring up at the proprietor, who didn't look any too happy with her.

"Are you having a fit or something?" she demanded.

Erin blew out a breath and tried to get her bearings. Coming out of a vision was always a little tiring and this time, she felt as though she'd been running a marathon.

"Huh? What? A fit?"

"What've you got? Amnesia?"

"No," Erin said and eased up on one elbow. "Why am I on the floor?"

"Because you tipped over in a dead faint," the woman said and the two elderly customers Erin had seen before each nodded in agreement.

"That's very true, dear," one of the ladies said with a brisk nod, "you did. Frightened me and my sister half to death."

"So," the proprietor said loudly, "if you think you're going to sue me for this, you can think again," the woman warned. "I've got surveillance cameras, young lady. And witnesses. You didn't trip over anything. You just toppled clean over."

Oh, for Heaven's sake.

"I'm not going to sue," Erin assured her and sat up slowly, since her stomach was a little on the icky side at the moment. Astral traveling always upset her stomach.

"It's closing time," the old woman, clearly not a people person said, "so I think you'd better go."

"Yeah." Erin picked the knife off the floor beside her warily, half expecting the visions to come again. But for the moment at least, the knife was quiet, as if it had shown her all it could and now she was on her own.

Well, that was fine. She at least had an idea of what to do now. Where to go.

Standing, she said, "I'd like to buy this before I go. How much?"

"I'll have to check," the cranky old woman said as her eyes lit up. She led the way to the cash register and Erin knew her VISA card was going to take a serious hit.

But that didn't matter. She'd found the man who could help her. She knew it instinctively. Just as she knew that though he had died centuries ago, Santos was alive now.

And Erin knew just where to find him.

San Diego, California.

Chapter 2

Santos stalked through the night, keeping his legendary focus directed solely at his target. The demon who had shimmered away from their fight early that morning. Better than trying to understand how that mysterious woman had suddenly appeared before him. Again.

He hadn't seen her in more than five hundred years. Hadn't experienced that flash of something molten sliding through his system. One look into her green eyes had thrown Santos off his guard—just as it had the night he'd died so long ago.

Who was she?

What did she want?

And where the hell had she gone?

"No matter," he said, willing himself to believe it. She was nothing to him. No more than a distraction, perhaps arranged by the very demons he fought.

As an Immortal Guardian, Santos, like his fellow warriors, possessed powers gifted to them by the beings who had first created them. It was the duty of every Guardian to guard the portals leading from the demon dimensions and to capture and return to their personal hell any demon who managed to escape into this reality.

And like Guardians, all demons were different. Each might have powers that others lacked. The demons were motivated to stay free of their dimension in order to kill, to spread dissension, to infiltrate humanity and create chaos.

The Guardians were all that stood between them and the mortal world.

Santos could not afford to be distracted from the job at hand. The small demon had escaped him earlier—after Santos had captured the demon's master. And though the small one was no great threat to humanity, its presence in this world was unacceptable.

"Little bastard," Santos muttered, slipping through an alley, barely noticing the stench of garbage spilling from one of the industrial-sized trash cans pushed flush against a brick wall. "What honor is there in running from a fight?"

But even as he thought it, Santos could admit to the irony in that statement. Demons? *Honor?* The two words had no business being in the same sentence.

And yet, in the more than five hundred years he had been fighting the underworld, he had found that even the most vicious of demons had their own "code." Not one that he or any of his fellow Guardians would ascribe to, but a code nonetheless.

Centuries of life and a steady stream of battles had taught Santos to never discount an opponent. So he was here, in the back alleys of downtown San Diego, following the trace energy patterns of the demon that had escaped him. He'd never failed to capture his target and he wasn't going to fail now.

His quiet, careful footsteps were lost in the noise of the city. A rat scuttled out of his way. Traffic hummed on the main streets and tourists laughed and chatted as they meandered along the sidewalks. None of those in the light could even guess at what was happening in the shadows.

But that was as it had always been. Those safe in their own comfortable little lives rarely took the time to glance around them at the darkness. Which ordinarily made his job that much easier.

He stopped suddenly at the mouth of the alley and lifted his gaze to the night sky. The moon was partially covered by clouds, allowing peaks of silver to shine through as brightly as diamonds. The stars were nearly invisible, lost in the harsh glare of the city lights. But did it matter? Humans so rarely looked outside themselves, he doubted many of them ever bothered to glance upward. Shaking his head, Santos stared down the sidewalk and looked past the crowds, searching for the demon's trail.

He could see nothing from his vantage point though, and moved to enter the crowd. But first Santos waved one hand, creating a wall of energy around himself that would hide him from all eyes. Now he could move through the people of this perpetually damp city without concern. No one here would ever know that an Immortal Guardian had walked among them. Had tracked and captured a demon bent on trouble. No one would have any idea that life was anything but ordinary.

He shook his head and took a deep breath of the sea-scented air. He'd had enough of this place.

The damp, cold air seeped into his bones. The never-ending crowd of tourists choked him. The tangle of homes and cars annoyed him. He longed for his home in Barcelona. There, even though he lived atop a cliff overlooking the ocean, the air was cool without the ever-cloying sense of wet. His blood was made for Spain. The heat, the searing sun and the sense of openness that was denied him here.

He averted his gaze from a homeless man staggering along behind his shopping cart and looked instead out at the night. San Diego might be thought of as a nice place to live but to Santos, it was merely another city, with a dark, dangerous underbelly like any other.

The moment he could, Santos would be taking his jet and flying home.

He'd only meant to remain in San Diego briefly. He had come up from Mexico, where he had followed a demon, expecting to go directly to the airport to fly his jet to Spain. Instead, Michael, the being who directed the Guardians, had asked him to stay.

The Guardian who had long protected San Diego, had finally chosen to end his existence. Pain whipped through Santos like a lash and then dissipated again. That Guardian, Stewart Marsh, had been a friend. A stalwart fighter. One who had held the demons at bay for three hundred years. Santos frowned at the loss, then let it go. There was no time. For pain. For remembrance. There was only battle.

Until Michael could assign someone else, this area was undefended. So it was Santos who must stand between the city and the dark.

"First, there is the matter of the demon." His dark eyes flashed as he scanned the motley crowd near the downtown bus station, searching for that soft pulse of colored energy that would lead him to his prey.

Finally, he spotted a pale wash of red stretched across the base of trees lining a postage-stamp-sized piece of green in the middle of downtown. It wasn't really a park. There wasn't enough of it for that. It was more an open spot not yet swallowed by the decaying buildings crouched alongside it.

For those who lived here, the empty lot with straggly bushes and a few spindly trees wouldn't mean much. But the demon was obviously trying to lose himself there.

Stepping out of the alley, Santos rushed into the street, never slowing for traffic. Instead, he simply leaped over the hoods of moving cars, their drivers completely unaware of him.

His blood quickened, and his heartbeat raced in anticipation of the coming fight. *This* was what made eternity worth living. Pitting his own strength against the demon world, one at a time. This was why he continued in an existence most men would have given up as empty centuries ago.

As his friend had.

To Santos, there was no other world but that of the warrior. He'd lived and died fighting and he would continue on doing so throughout time.

He moved through small swatches of pale yellow thrown from the street lights. He slipped into the tree line, no more than a barren square. This was what passed for countryside in the city. This tiny plot of ground where trees tried to survive and grass was parched and brown. Where straggly bushes bent in an icy wind. Santos sneered and once again allowed himself a brief memory of home.

The brown hills, the craggy mountains scraping the sky. The winding paths a man could wander and taste freedom. The sun spilling out of a brassy sky. The wide open expanse of land surrounding his mountaintop home. And the crash of the waves against the rocks below. Room enough for a man to breathe. He missed it with a soul-deep ache.

A rustle of sound caught his attention and Santos stopped. Lifting his head, he tasted the wind and smiled. Turning right, he crouched, moving along the gnarled bushes until he came to the final hibiscus. Gaudy pink flowers bloomed among the dusty green leaves, but he wasn't interested in the plant, only in what lay beneath it.

"You try my patience, small one."

"I'm not going back, Guardian." The bush rattled again as though the demon were trying to scramble even deeper into its cover of leaves. As if that would protect it. "I've done nothing to make you hunt me down this way."

Santos shrugged. He'd heard desperate pleas from his prey before and hadn't been moved to mercy. This time would be no different. "You are here, demon. Where you do not belong. That is enough."

The hibiscus swayed with a violent motion and suddenly the small, dark demon was standing in front of him. Like humans, every demon was different. There were those who were the stuff of nightmares—and there were those like this one. Annoying yes, but hardly evil.

"Your master has already been returned to its hell." That was a fight to remember, he thought, his blood stirring at the memory. The demon had fought with teeth and claws and a raw desperation. This creature would not provide such diversion. "You must follow."

"Forget you saw me," it whispered frantically "and I'll disappear. I'll get out of your territory."

Santos laughed and damn, it felt good. It wasn't often he ended a hunt with humor. "Demon, this *world* is my territory," he said, though that wasn't exactly the strictest truth. "And you are not a part of it."

"I'll fight."

"Good," Santos said, reaching for the sword in the scabbard at his side. "I had thought when you ran from me this morning that you had no honor. I am glad to see I was mistaken."

The demon was a foot shorter than Santos and its long black hair hung nearly to the ground. Its legs were short and bowed and its arms thick with muscle. Its dark red eyes locked on Santos as it mused, "I could shimmer again. You wouldn't be able to find me. Why not just let me go, save us both the trouble?"

Santos sighed. "You tire me. I thought you

would fight like a—" he broke off and let that sentence fade.

"Like a *man?*" Clearly furious, the demon backed up, one slow step at a time. "You insult me."

"And you waste my time." Santos swung his sword out in a wide arc and the little demon tried to shimmer away again. This time though, Santos was ready for it. Attaching a net of finely spun silver webbing to the edge of his sword, he'd dropped it over the demon before it could move. Once caught in a Guardian's net, a demon was helpless and powerless to escape.

"You should have fought me," Santos said as he slid his sword back into its scabbard and reached down to tighten the net around his catch. "It would have been the honorable thing to do."

The demon squirmed and kicked and snarled, but was unable to do anything beyond hurl insults and threats at the man who had caught it.

"I'll only escape again," it promised, its voice scraping the night air like broken glass. "And when I do, I'll find you and kill you."

"That has been tried before." Santos swung the demon over his shoulder and walked out of the city's pitiful excuse for a park. Moving through the shadows, Santos headed for his car. It wouldn't take long to drive to the closest demon dimension portal.

There were many—each leading to any number of hells. But the energy trace surrounding every demon was a signature of sorts—preventing demons from moving from one hellish world to another. Once returned to a portal, the demon had no choice but to return to the world from which it had come.

"If only the gods had chosen to seal the portals into this world," Santos mused aloud, then reconsidered. If they had done that, what would a warrior have to do?

"I will kill you, Guardian. This I swear. I will find you and tear out your liver. I will wear your eyeballs on my hat. I will—"

"Cease, demon!" Santos bellowed. "Your threats mean nothing. But should you ever manage to escape again—when you come looking for me," he said, "come to Spain. There we will have a fight for the ages, small one."

He was close.

Erin could feel him.

She'd spent the last hour driving up and down the streets of San Diego, letting the ivory-handled knife lead her. There'd been no more visions, but the deeply carved handle was still warm to the touch and still filled her with an urgency she was in no position to argue with.

It was also sort of like radar. Every time she turned the wrong way, she felt a sense of loss. But if she was going in the right direction, a sense of rightness welled up inside her. As if the knife were leading her to its original owner.

Her eyes felt gritty and every bone in her body wept with fatigue. She'd been on the move since leaving Maine the day before for New York City. She'd taken a red eye out of La Guardia, landed at LAX and rented a car. Two hours later she'd arrived in San Diego.

The day was gorgeous. Full clouds sailing across an achingly blue sky. Erin watched late-season tourists headed for the zoo or for Sea World with more than a little envy. She wished she were on a mission of fun. She wished she could have her life back. Heck. She just wished she could lay down somewhere and fall asleep for a day or two. This staying awake for twenty-four hours was nuts.

But she couldn't sleep. Couldn't relax her guard. Not until she had some answers. Not until she knew no one was going to attack her in her sleep.

With the knife on her lap, she steered her rental
car down a street that led off the Coast Highway.
Heat from the knife burned her thighs right
through the fabric of her jeans. She was going the
right way.

Huge old trees leaned across the street toward
each other in a leafy arch that even the sun
couldn't penetrate. He was even closer now. She
sensed his presence. Steering her car down the
slope, she came to a small private road.

She drove slowly along the tree-lined street,
reaching for the knife and keeping it tight in her
left hand. The warmth of the ivory comforted her.
Odd, but true. The shadowy road wound its way
down a steep hill. People were out walking their
dogs, washing their cars, enjoying the afternoon.

The houses she passed were amazing. Some
were just cottages, probably had been there for
fifty years. But others had blossomed and grown
into mansions—of every different type. There
were Tudors cuddled alongside Spanish style.
There were brick homes and clapboard and even
one with a conical tower that made Erin think
wistfully of fairy tales.

She followed the curve of the road, going
slowly, knowing she was close. She'd been so

intent on getting here, she hadn't really planned on what she'd say to the man once she was face-to-face with the mysterious Santos. Her stomach was jittery and the palms of her hands were damp. If he couldn't help her, she didn't know what she would do.

With a sudden sense of certainty, she parked her rental car across the street from the house she knew belonged to Santos. Number twelve.

"He will help," she told herself, taking a quick look in the rearview mirror. She pinched her pale cheeks, fluffed her shoulder-length, dark red hair, and then sighed. She'd been awake and on the run for twenty-four hours. No way was a pinch and a fluff going to make her presentable.

"So stop stalling already." She nodded. "Right."

She tossed a quick glance at her goal. The house behind number twelve sat far back from the road, protected by more trees. There were several other houses here and lots of cars parked on the street. So she should be safe enough. Even if her stalker had followed her, he couldn't have gotten here *before* her.

"Just do this, Erin. Go see the man. Tell him what's going on. *Make* him help you."

She grabbed her purse off the passenger seat,

tossed the knife inside and stepped out of the car. With her gaze fixed on the house in front of her, she shut the car door and started across the street.

From a distance, she heard a car engine fire to life and shriek as the driver gunned it hard. Heart racing, she gulped in air, turned her head toward the sound and froze. A low-slung red car hurtled toward her. Tires squealing, engine roaring, it raced forward.

Erin tried to move. She really did. But it was as if she were hypnotized. Not just by the car. But by the latest in a series of attacks. How many more times could she survive? How much longer could she remain alert?

And how could she defend herself against an enemy that went unnamed?

"Look out!" A man's voice. Close by.

She'd hardly registered his presence before he was charging into her. His momentum carried them both out of the path of the car as he wrapped both arms around her and pushed her to safety.

She hit the asphalt hard.

Her hip took most of it, but her shoulder, too, screamed with pain. The car raced by them, never slowing, never stopping.

"Thank you." She turned her head on the street

to face her rescuer. But he was gone. Twisting painfully, she caught a glimpse of him—a tall man with blond hair—running down the street and disappearing around a bend. "What the *hell* is going on?"

"That, madam," another deep voice sounded out from above, "is what I would like to know."

Chapter 3

Erin looked up.

Way up.

Her gaze traveled the length of long muscular legs, wearing black slacks with a knife edge crease. Up past a flat abdomen and a broad chest covered by an open-throated, long-sleeved white shirt. Up beyond a square, hard jaw, a proud nose that had been broken at least once and into flat, dark eyes that stared, unblinking, down at her.

"Santos."

He frowned, glanced up and down the street, then shifted his gaze back to her. "You again. How do you know my name? Who are you? What are you doing here?"

Erin pushed herself into a sitting position, dusted the palms of her hands together to get rid of the gravel biting into her skin, then glared right back at him. "I've come a long way to find you."

"That explains nothing." He set fisted hands on his hips.

She was tired, dirty, sore and oh, yes, *terrified.* So she wasn't exactly feeling polite when she said, "I'll explain everything. Later. Right now, I'd like to recover from someone just trying to run me down in the street."

He nodded and shot a look in the direction the car had disappeared. "I saw it. I couldn't reach you in time—"

"Someone did," she pointed out.

"I saw that, as well."

"You had quite the view, then."

"Who are you?"

"Erin Brady," she said and held one hand out toward him.

He looked at it for a long moment before grabbing it and yanking her to her feet in one smooth motion. "And I am Ricardo Esteban Amadeo Santos."

"Wow." She'd known the Santos part, but his whole name was magical and musical and…back on track, Erin.

"You have told me your name, woman. Not who you are."

But Erin hardly heard him. At the first touch of his hand on hers, her mind had erupted with images. Visions rushed through her brain and she held her breath as she experienced them all in a heartbeat of time.

She and Santos. In bed. Limbs tangled on ivory sheets. His mouth on hers. His hands caressing. She felt the need swell within and heat filled her center, making her knees weak and her breath catch in her throat.

She tried to pull free, but his fingers tightened on hers. And in the space of a breath, the sultry, sexual images faded. Terrifying images swamped her. *Darkness. Shifting shadows. Glittering knives. A palace of black stone that shone like obsidian under the light of an orange moon.* Memory? One of his memories? They didn't feel like memories though, and that scared her.

Erin swayed with the power rocketing through her.

"Woman?"

She couldn't hear him.

Couldn't hear anything but the screams rising up from the shadows in her mind.

Santos watched the woman's eyes roll back in her head. Moving quickly, he caught her before she smacked down hard against the street. He heard each wrenching breath torn from her lungs and knew he couldn't ignore her. Though truth be told, he would not have left her on the street anyway. Not until he discovered just who the hell she was and how she had come to haunt him, not only now but five hundred years before.

He looked down into her face and felt the strength of the connection that had been forged long ago. On the night of his death. When she had appeared to him on the heaving deck of the *Niña*, he'd thought at first she was an angel. A portent of death. And since he had died only moments after seeing her, that seemed a reasonable assumption.

Her features had danced through his dreams for centuries. Taunting, teasing, smiling at him in a way a woman does when desire takes her.

Santos swept the woman into his arms and simply held on to her for a long moment. His heartbeat hammered in his chest. His breath rushed in and out of his lungs. The woman from his dreams. Impossible to believe she was here. Warm and real and in his arms. The woman he'd seen the night he died. The woman who only yesterday had appeared before him on a city street.

He held her closer and narrowed his gaze. Instinct had him searching the area with a slow, thorough scan. But there was nothing out of the ordinary. The man who had saved her from the speeding car had disappeared as quickly as the threat.

He sniffed the air, but found no trace of a demon nearby. Finally, he shifted his gaze back to the woman lying unconscious in his grasp. She was short and curvy and her breasts rose and fell with her even breathing. He wanted her to wake up. Wanted to look into those emerald-green eyes again.

Wanted to know who the devil she was.

"Soon," he whispered and bent to scoop her purse off the asphalt. Then he stalked to the drive, holding his own personal phantom close.

The magical wards set up around the perimeter of the property strained as he passed through them. Strong enough to keep out any demon that might try to invade the Guardian's home, the protection spell allowed passage to all but the demon realm. Now, he thought that perhaps he should arrange for stronger wards. To keep out all but he and those who worked for him.

Moments ago, he'd been standing on the balcony of the great house hidden in the trees. He had seen the woman start across the street. Seen the car burst into life and charge at her—aiming directly at her. Seen the man come out of nowhere to push her to safety. All in a matter of seconds. He had been too far away to reach her and in that heartbeat of time, he'd felt more helpless—more powerless than ever before in his life. A man used to action, to protecting mortals, he had been forced to watch as a young woman faced her death. Only to see her survive.

At the memory, his arms tightened around her, pressing her body closer to his. He'd had no idea then that she was the woman he had dreamt of for centuries. No idea that she was somehow even *more* than that.

From the first instant he touched her, he'd felt it. A rush of…expectation. Of destiny. He wanted to shake it off, but that bone-deep realization would not fade. It was the sure and steady sense that nothing in his life would ever be the same again after today. That this woman was going to bring chaos and wonder into a world that had become commonplace.

But there was a part of him that resented her very presence. His life was as he had made it. As he wanted it. Introducing a woman—even *this* woman—into it was only asking for trouble.

She stirred as he crossed the meticulously kept lawn. Her amazing eyes opened and fixed on him. And for one brief moment, Santos indulged himself by looking into the depths of those eyes.

Then she spoke and the spell was shattered.

"Where are we going?"

His jaw tightened and his spine stiffened. He was a Guardian. No man to be waylaid by the promise of deep green eyes and a lush body. "My home."

"Oh," she said on a grateful sigh, "good."

One eyebrow lifted. As much as he felt a connection to her, he was not ready to dismiss centuries of suspicion. "Do not think yourself a guest quite yet, woman. There are questions that must be answered."

"That's okay." She cuddled in trustingly close to him, making his body fire with a need he couldn't quash. "I can do that. All I need is a little sleep. Then I'll be good to go. Really…"

Her eyes closed again before he reached the front door and anything he might have said died unuttered. Santos stopped dead in the middle of the yard. A cold, damp sea breeze swept past him, lifting her hair into a swirl of dark red flame about her head. He shouldn't take her into the house, he knew. She wasn't a demon. He knew that much, as there was no wash of trace energy clinging to her. But she might be in league with a demon. She could be the Trojan horse, sent to invade his sanctuary—seduce him into compliance so that—

As soon as the thought rushed through his mind, Santos threw back his head and laughed. Yes, he wanted her. Yes, his body already hungered for hers, as if every cell of his being had suddenly wakened to a ferocious need. But the idea that Ricardo Esteban Amadeo Santos could be turned from his duty by the beauty of a woman was absurd. Shaking his head, his laughter faded slowly as he studied her.

"If it is your plan to trap me with desire, woman," he whispered, "be warned. I'm not a man to be led by his cock. I will have answers from you or—dream woman or not—you will find yourself back in the street where I found you."

He headed for the house again with long, sure

strides. Santos kicked one of the oak panels and waited impatiently until it swung open. A tall, dark-haired man with pale blue eyes, wearing jeans and a gray sweater looked at him, shocked. "Is she injured?"

Thomas Hawthorn and his wife Amy had arrived only three weeks before from England. They and their families had worked for Guardians most of their lives. They knew exactly who and what Santos was and did all they could to assist him.

"She will not remain awake long enough for me to determine that," Santos admitted. He carried her easily down the marble hall to the wide staircase. As he started up, he glanced back at the man still watching him. "Please ask Amy to make some tea. If I can wake her up, I'm sure she will appreciate it."

"Yes, sir."

Santos barely heard him. He took the carpeted stairs two at a time, his footsteps muffled in the stillness of the vast mansion. This opulent palace by a cold sea would never feel like home to him, though even Santos could concede that it was more than adequate. Pale ivory walls were dotted by framed works of art. A thick, dark red carpet runner stretched along the long hall, covering the gleaming oak floorboards and lending richness to the surroundings.

But Santos paid none of it any attention. He hit the second-floor landing, turned left and walked directly to the master bedroom.

He could have used one of the guest rooms, but until he knew who and what this woman was, he planned on keeping her close. Even if that meant in his own bed.

Weak afternoon sunlight washed through the sheer white curtains drawn across the French doors leading to a stone patio that overlooked the back garden and the ocean beyond. A massive dark oak bed was pushed against one wall and opposite it was a huge stone fireplace with two plush armchairs pulled up before the now cold hearth.

Santos walked directly to the bed and laid her out on top of the pale blue silk duvet. He reached down to pull off her tennis shoes, then moved back to the head of the bed. She moaned, whispered something he didn't catch and turned onto her side, facing him.

Her long, dark red hair lay in tumbled curls around her shoulders and across her face. In sharp contrast, her fair skin seemed even paler than it should have. There were bruised shadows beneath her eyes and the soft sigh that escaped her told him just how tired she was.

Something inside him stirred again and he didn't look too closely at the sensation. If it was pity, so be it. But he would remain in control of this situation. He would not allow a woman—no matter how beautiful—to turn him from the duty that was first and foremost in his life.

"Sleep then." He couldn't resist reaching out to lift her hair away from her face. And if his fingers rubbed the silky strands, who would know? When he straightened, he said, "But when you wake, I will be expecting those answers you promised me."

Erin woke with a jolt.

She sat straight up and looked around wildly, half expecting some new threat to come flying at her from the corners of the room. That's when her gaze landed on the man she'd come so far to find.

Sitting in a chair at the far side of the bed, his arms were folded across his broad chest and his legs were crossed, one booted foot resting on a knee. His dark eyes were fixed on her and his features were hard. Expressionless.

If she had been hoping for comfort, she wasn't going to find it here.

But that was all right. She didn't need her hand held. What she needed was help in finding out what was happening before it was too late.

"When I was asleep, I dreamed I met you," she said and her voice was almost lost in the cavernous room.

"This was no dream."

"No," she said as aches and pains began to make themselves known. This was all too real. Her hip throbbed from where she'd landed on it in the street and the palms of her hands were scraped red and raw. Plus, her stomach was rumbling, reminding her that she hadn't eaten in hours. Or was it days?

Beyond him, curtains were pushed back to show that night had fallen. An icy wind swept through the opened French doors and in the sky, stars shone down with cold indifference.

"How long have I been asleep?"

"Hours." One word. Clipped.

"I was tired." Exhausted would be a better word, but he didn't need to know that she hadn't had a decent night's sleep in weeks. Shoving one hand through her hair, she pushed it back from her

face and let her gaze slide from his. He was too
intense. Too…focused on her. Her body stirred
under his direct stare and she didn't want to think
about that at the moment.

Instead, she took another look at the room
where he'd brought her. A fire burned in a stone
hearth and before the fire rested a small table in
front of a pair of bloodred wingback chairs. On the
table rested a covered dish and her stomach
growled again, this time loud enough for him to
hear it.

From the side of the bed, Santos sighed and
she whipped her head around to look at him.
"You are hungry?"

"Starving," she admitted. What was the point
of denying it?

"There are cold sandwiches," he said, lifting
one shoulder in a careless shrug. "The tea is no
doubt long cold, but I will arrange for more."

"Thanks, but more tea is not necessary." She
scooted off the bed on the opposite side from him.
He wasn't looking any too friendly and she needed
something to eat before delving into the reasons
why she was here.

Heading for the table, she lifted the silver cover
off the plate and almost groaned upon seeing the

thick, roast beef sandwiches. Grabbing up a half of one, she took a big bite, then turned abruptly as she sensed him directly behind her.

She almost bumped right into him. In her defense, he took up a lot of room. Up close, his shoulders and chest were even broader than she remembered from her first glimpse of him. His eyes burned with a dark fire that seemed to singe every nerve ending in her body.

Erin swallowed hard, took a breath and said, "God, you move quiet."

"So I have been told."

"Could you back up a little? You're making me nervous." Not completely true, she thought. He was making her a lot more than nervous. She hadn't expected this. Hadn't been prepared for the rise of desire so thick it nearly choked her. She hadn't anticipated the incredible want building inside her. And she wasn't entirely sure what to do with it. She needed his help. She didn't need him in her bed.

Keep that in mind, Erin. She took another bite of the truly excellent roast beef, chewed and swallowed, stalling for time.

"I can wait. Take as long as you like to eat and drink, to regain your senses. But you will not leave

this room until I know why you are here. And
how you come to appear before me at odd moments with no warning."

God, that voice. Soft and dark and compelling.
He spoke with an Old World sort of formality,
which tugged at something inside her. Plus, there
was the accent. A hint of Spanish flavored his
words and made him all the more hard to resist.
He could probably have been a very successful
hypnotist or something. Send women into
hormone-driven comas just by speaking.

"Do you hear me?"

"Yeah. I hear you." All too well. That voice of
his was a weapon, designed to bring women to
their knees. And boy, did it work well.

She took a breath and tightened her hold on
the sandwich. Get a grip on yourself, Erin. She
couldn't afford to be distracted by the lush swell
of sexual attraction—though God, it wasn't easy
to ignore. Still, he was right. Stalling was pointless. After all, she'd come a long way to talk to
this man. In her vision, she had felt unerringly
that *he* was the one person who would be able
to help her.

Forcing herself to look up into his eyes, she
fought to not lose herself in those dark depths

swirling with impatience and suspicion. Because strength was also there. Strength she needed.

So much had happened over the last few weeks. She had felt herself surrendering to fear that seemed to color every breath she took. And now, when she had finally found the one man she was sure could keep her alive, she had to throw caution to the wind. She had to take a firm stand. Tell him who she was and what she needed. Then she would tell him that she knew he would help her.

Because *he* had a secret he protected.

And thanks to her visions, she knew what that secret was.

Chapter 4

Santos's eyes narrowed on her and his jaw twitched as his teeth ground together. Erin felt a flutter of nerves, but stiffened her spine in response. She'd been through a lot in her life and had never backed down like some gutless weenie. She couldn't afford to start now.

When he spoke again, his voice rumbled with the deep-throated power of some caged lion—a *hungry* caged lion. "What is this secret you believe you know?"

Erin staggered back a step. How did he know what she'd been thinking? "Excuse me?"

"You believe I have a secret and you wish to use this against me in some way?"

"Okay, that's just weird." She pulled in a breath and tried to steady herself, but it was pointless, she knew. She'd been on edge for weeks now and the most recent attempt on her life hadn't helped any. If that stranger hadn't shown up out of nowhere, she'd be nothing more than a spot on the pavement by now.

But putting that aside for the moment... What kind of man was she dealing with here? Had he looked into her mind and plucked out her thoughts? No. Ridiculous. Mind reading wasn't real.

Which almost made her laugh. After all, she could touch any object and sense its history, its past, its owners' lives and deaths. But *mind reading* wasn't real?

Shaking his head, he said, "I can read your face easily, woman. Your eyes flash with every thought and your every expression reveals those thoughts."

"They don't do either," she said, but shifted her gaze just in case.

Unexpectedly, he laughed and the sound seemed to boom out around them, echoing off the walls. She couldn't help it. She looked at him again and her breath caught in her throat. Dour and dangerous, the man was amazing looking. With a grin on his face, he was simply overwhelming.

Erin's heartbeat sped up into a rhythm that had her reaching out to lay one hand on the back of the closest chair just to keep her balance. He was more than she'd imagined he would be. And suddenly, she wasn't so sure anymore if coming here had been such a great idea.

He was powerful and clearly rich and the look in his eyes when his laughter died away made her knees weak. Oh, boy.

"You are a poor liar," he said with a brief nod. "Which is good. It tells me you are not used to it."

"You're right," she said. "I'm not." Setting her half-eaten sandwich down, she briskly rubbed her palms up and down her arms. But it didn't help. The sensation of cold she'd carried with her for the last few weeks remained as strong as ever. And the heat she felt from him wasn't the kind to bring her peace. No, it carried its own sense of danger.

Beside her, the fire crackled and hissed, sparks shooting up the chimney in flaring bursts. Warmth reached for her, but couldn't touch the cold within. Nothing could. It was fear. She knew that. She'd been living on a razor's edge for weeks and fear had become her closest companion. One she would willingly get rid of. If she could.

"You're shivering."

"I know."

Frowning, he stalked over to a set of double doors and disappeared inside what was probably the biggest walk-in closet she'd ever seen. When he came back out, he was carrying a heavy black sweater that he handed to her without comment.

"Thanks." Erin slipped it on over her head and inhaled the scent of him as she did. And there was more. In a brief flurry of images, she saw him, *wearing that sweater, standing on a balcony, staring up at the stars. She saw him walking along the beach, the wind in his hair, a sword in his hand.*

Her heart twisted unexpectedly as she felt his loneliness and a part of her responded to it. Hadn't she been mostly alone her whole life? But she couldn't feel sympathy for the man she'd come to blackmail into helping her.

She eased the visions away with a practiced mental "push" and took another deep breath in the hopes of steadying herself. It was a futile hope though, and she knew it. How could she find balance in her life when everything was falling apart around her? No, the only way to find her way back to the normal, everyday world she'd created for herself was to uncover the danger to her. By facing it down. By defeating the threat.

And to do that, she needed him.

Pulling her hair free and letting it hang down her back, she faced him and blurted, "I need your help."

One dark eyebrow lifted. "And why should I help you?"

"Because of that secret of yours."

"I have no secrets."

"You're a poor liar, too."

He frowned at her and coming from someone else, that glacial expression might have scared her. But she felt no threat coming from him. Her senses would have picked up on that the moment she had touched him. The moment he handed her a sweater. He wasn't the most patient man in the world, but he wasn't a danger to her.

Knowing that gave her the courage to simply blurt out the truth.

"I know you're not human," she said and lifted her chin, silently daring him to call her a liar again.

He surprised her by not only not denying it, but offering a challenge of his own.

"And you are?" he countered. "The first time I saw you was five hundred years ago."

"I know—"

"And then again yesterday."

"Yes, and—"

"Each time, you appeared out of nowhere and vanished again in the space of a single heartbeat."

"It was a vision."

Santos folded his arms over his broad chest and looked down at her with a gleam in his eye that ordered her to continue.

Erin couldn't seem to draw a steady breath while standing so close to him, so she started walking. She paced the perimeter of the lushly appointed bedroom—no doubt *his*—and talked as she walked.

"I have this 'gift,' at least that's what people call it, though it's not a gift anyone would ask for, believe me. And if I could return it, I seriously would. But the thing is, I touch something and I can see its past. I can see where it's been, who has owned it, what happened to those people."

"I see."

She didn't even look at him. She'd had people laugh at her before, so hey, not in any hurry to experience that again, thanks very much. Nobody believed her, really. Well, her adoptive father finally had, but that hadn't been such a good thing. She was sixteen the night he dropped his jacket on the floor in the hall.

Erin had picked it up and the images that had crashed into her mind had shown him at a casino, buying a stack of chips with his paycheck while holding a big-chested blonde on his lap. When he saw her shocked face, he knew that she knew and from that night on, he'd made her life so miserable that she'd finally run away a year later. Her adoptive mother was no help. She'd long since considered Erin a freak. And she had been all too willing to let Erin go.

So, Erin had learned to keep her little psychic power to herself. Until tonight, she'd told only one other person in her life. Jack Baker had been her first real love. The man who hired her as assistant chef in his restaurant. The man she'd thought loved her.

Erin stopped dead, shook her head hard enough to make her hair fly out about her head and told herself to stop thinking about the damn past. There was nothing to be done. Nothing to change. And unless she focused on what was happening here, she'd never have a future.

"I was in Maine a couple of days ago," she said

and shot him a quick look as she paused by the open French doors. Staring out at the night and the starlit sky, she inhaled the sea-scented air and told herself to just get it over with. "I found an ivory-handled knife in an antique store. I picked it up and I saw *you*."

She looked at him again and noticed that he'd moved, silently, stealthily. He was close to her now, but his features were in shadow. She couldn't see his eyes, and maybe that was for the best. One look into those fathomless depths and she might just lose what nerve she had left.

"On the ship," he whispered, his voice no more than a breath.

"Yes." The memories were so vivid, she could still hear the men screaming, the groan of the ship as it struggled to stay afloat. "I've had these visions all my life, but that one was…different."

"Because I saw you."

"Yes. That's never happened before." And she still didn't know what to make of that.

He moved in closer, stepping from the shadows into a wash of moonlight slanting through the French doors. His dark eyes glittered, and Erin felt something inside her shiver.

"And yesterday?"

"It was the same vision, only a fast forward to the present. I don't know why," she admitted, then met his gaze and said, "but when I realized you were alive, I knew I had to find you. I *knew* that you were the man who could help me."

"You say that as if it has already been decided."

"It has." She swallowed hard and said, "If you don't help me, I'll go to the media. I'll tell them what I know. That you're not who you claim to be. That you *died* five hundred years ago."

He smiled, but the curve of his mouth had nothing to do with humor. "No one will believe you. What you say is impossible."

Oh, she knew that. And she knew he was right. Most people wouldn't believe her. She'd caught on to that by the time she was five or six. In fact, the general consensus would probably be that she was the crazy one. "But even if only a few believe me, your secret will be out."

"You think to gain my help with threats?" he asked and the menace in his voice should have frightened her. But she'd had plenty of scares over the last few weeks. She must be getting used to them.

"I don't have anything else to bargain with." Erin turned her back on him, more to avoid

looking into those eyes of his again than for any
other reason. Then she walked out onto the stone
patio and realized instantly that she was still
wearing only her socks. The cold of the stone
seeped up through the soles of her feet and swirled
together with the constant cold within to make
her feel as though she'd been carved from ice.

The hunter waited in the trees, patient, deter-
mined. He must take care of the woman tonight.
The signs were clear. If she was not eliminated—
soon—the world itself was in peril. Damn, the car
should have worked. The woman should be dead
now and the world safe.

Hunching deeper into the camouflage the leafy
tree presented, he stared at the big house over-
looking the ocean and let his rage build. She
shouldn't have made it to the Guardian. She was
supposed to have died in Maine, far from any help
the Immortal might offer. But, he told himself, it
wouldn't matter in the long run. The Guardian
would fail. Anyone who stood between them and
the death of the woman would fail.

They had to.

The woman must die. He would have pre-
ferred that death to look like an accident—and

*yet, dead was dead. What did it matter really
how she met her end?*

As long as it happened soon.

Erin didn't hear his steps as Santos followed
her out onto the balcony, but she knew he was
right behind her. The heat of his body seemed to
shimmer all around her. He had a presence she'd
never encountered before. She didn't have a lot of
experience with men in general, but she had the
distinct impression that all the experience in the
world wouldn't have prepared her for *him*.

"What is it you want me to do?" he asked.

She splayed her hands on the carved stone
railing, digging her nails into the pebbly surface.
Knowing that he was at least willing to listen to
her gave Erin the chance to draw the first easy
breath she had in weeks. Staring off into the night,
she looked past the garden that lay in shadows to
the ocean beyond. Moonlight lay across the
surface of the water like a silver path, waiting for
those who knew how to follow it.

"I need you to help me find out who my father is.
Why he wants me dead. And to help me stay alive."

"The car today was an attempt, then?"

"And a bus in Brooklyn," she said on a sigh,

"and a falling sign in Queens, and someone was following me in Maine, too."

"You live in Maine?"

"No," she said, still looking out at the night. "I live in Manhattan—but I grew up here. Well, in Orange County."

"And why is someone trying to kill you?"

"It sounds so weird, even I have a hard time believing it," she admitted, then kept talking, since she had his attention. "I got a letter five years ago. From my birth mother."

"And?"

She glanced at him, then looked away. Seriously, staring into his eyes was nearly hypnotic. And she so didn't need that at the moment. "In the letter, she said that my father—don't know who he is, before you ask—was going to steal my psychic power and kill me on my thirtieth birthday."

"You believe this to be true?" He wasn't laughing at her. Wasn't calling her a nutcase. That was something, at least.

"I didn't at first. But…" She turned and faced him, trying very hard not to look into his eyes. "I turn thirty in three weeks. And just a few weeks ago, being me became really dangerous."

"That is when these attempts on your life began?"

"Yeah." She blew out a breath. "I don't know what to do. I don't know who my father is. Don't know why he wants to kill me—" A short bark of laughter shot from her throat and she slapped one hand over her mouth to keep hysteria from escaping. When she felt as though she could speak without keening, she chanced a look into his eyes. "I don't want to die."

He closed the distance between them and laid one huge hand on her shoulder.

Sex. Amazing sex. At the touch of his hand, her mind raced with image after image. *Erin groaned as Santos's hands slid up and down her naked body, caressing, stroking, teasing her into a frenzy of need that had her screaming his name. His mouth took hers and his tongue claimed her with a fierceness she'd never known. His breath became hers. His heartbeat pounded in time with hers. His body entered hers, hard and deep, again and again and...*

"What is it?" he demanded, giving her shoulder a shake that had Erin snapping out of the vision that had left her body on fire and her mind a scramble.

"Oh, God." She backed up and away from him, shaking her head, struggling for air. God, why couldn't she breathe? "Don't. Just, don't touch me. I can't believe this, I don't know why it's happening, I shouldn't be picking up anything from you. It doesn't *happen* with people. Only objects. And even with objects, it doesn't happen all the time." She snorted a choked-off laugh. "Maybe I'm finally actually losing my mind. Maybe everybody was right and I *am* crazy…"

Guardians were telepaths, so Santos could pick out the occasional thought from this woman's rambling, disorganized mind. Which was how he'd known that she was planning to blackmail him into helping her. Just a moment ago, he'd read her terror clearly in her thoughts. But now, her mind was such a jumble, Santos didn't have a clue what she'd seen when he touched her that had so upset her. But this woman was getting to him despite his better instincts.

He knew that at least part of what she'd said was true. He had seen her in a vision. Twice. He had been a part of whatever she had been experiencing. So her story of finding his knife—which he would like back—made a strange sort of sense.

But this… Why would a father, especially one who had never met his child, want her dead?

In the next instant, every sense he had went on alert.

"Get down!" He grabbed her even as he spoke. Throwing her to the stone floor, Santos felt a hot, punch of pain in his right shoulder and less than a heartbeat later, the report of a rifle echoed off the stillness and shattered the quiet.

He hissed in a breath and lifted his head, his eyes narrowed in fury. It wasn't the first time Santos had been shot and most probably would not be the last. Demons used whatever weapon came to hand to fight for their freedom. But this time, it wasn't *he* who had been the target. His senses had picked out the threat only a bare instant before the attacker had fired. If he hadn't been beside her—

Erin lay beneath him, stunned and terrified. Covering her body with his, Santos willed her to be silent and hoped it would work. Her green eyes were wide with shock as she stared up at him. Her chest rose and fell with each rapid breath and she bit at her bottom lip to keep from screaming. He felt her terror as his own. Felt her body tremble.

Felt the press of her body curving against his.

"Remain silent. Stay here." It was an order. He had no time for niceties.

And she apparently did not take orders well.

"That was a *shot*. Someone shot at me. Someone is *shooting* a *gun* at me. For God's sake, what's going on?" Her voice crept higher and higher with each word. Her fear was taking over. He saw it in her eyes and felt it in the sudden tension gripping her body.

"Silence." His voice was no more than a whispered shout, demanding her attention. He was concentrating on the threat, listening, tuning every sense out into the night, to determine if she were safe.

Every instinct had him clamoring to leap off the balcony and race into the night. Hunt down the threat and dispose of it. But he couldn't leave her alone. It wasn't safe.

"No, no. Get off me. You have to get off. We have to get out of here, we—"

He kissed her. It was the surest way he knew to shut her up fast. His mouth came down on hers and what began as a simple thing to solve an immediate problem, quickly became something else entirely.

Her mouth beneath his was pliant, soft,

tempting. At first, she tried to pull free, but Santos gave her no room to back away. Every cell in his body demanded that he hold her closer, tighter. He felt the pull of her and knew that there was more at work here than simple need. Simple attraction for a beautiful woman.

He *had* to taste her. Had to have more of her. Something stirred within, hungry, demanding, urging him to claim her. To take her.

And still, his warrior instincts clamored to be heard. Reluctantly, he lifted his head from hers and in that one split second, reached out into the darkness again, searching, scanning for imminent danger. But there was nothing. Whoever the shooter had been, he was gone.

Santos should have gotten up, taken Erin off the cold stones and taken her inside where he knew she would be safe. His wound meant nothing. As an Immortal, he couldn't be killed, and his body healed itself fairly quickly. And yet, moving from this spot could not have been further from his thoughts.

"You kissed me."

"Yes," he said and smiled at her. Her mouth was ripe and lush, her lips swollen from his kiss and when her tongue smoothed across her bottom lip, he felt raw, aching hunger. "And I plan to again."

She sucked in air, gulped it down hard, then blew it out again. "Okay then. Good."

He smiled down at her, then lowered his head to hers. He parted her lips with his tongue and groaned into her mouth at the first slick caress of her tongue against his. Here was something he hadn't expected.

A woman's mouth was a treasure to a man, yes. But this woman was something else. Something more. This woman caused every sense to light, pulsate. She was breath and life and temptation all packed into a small, curvy form designed to drive every thought but possessing her from a man's mind.

He cupped one hand behind her neck, holding her head still while he kissed her deeply, completely, giving and taking more than he ever had before. Her hands came up and around him, flattening against his back, holding him to her, scraping up and down his spine, making his blood quicken and his body swell to the point of bursting.

But when her hands smoothed across his shoulder and he hissed, she stopped. *You were shot.*

"Yes," he whispered aloud, responding to her thoughts instinctively.

You're bleeding.

Again, her thoughts came to him, clearly, as if she were speaking.

"It is nothing," he assured her, pausing to answer her unspoken questions between nibbles of the mouth he found endlessly tempting.

He wished she would stop speaking and give herself up to him. The pain in his shoulder was nothing. The fact that she was still an unknown to him meant nothing. There was something here he wanted to explore. Whatever danger there might be, could be faced tomorrow.

For now, tonight, there was only the two of them and the endless pleasures he would show her.

She pulled her mouth from his, slapped both hands against his broad chest and shoved. Hard.

"Endless pleasures?" She repeated his thoughts. "What was that? You think I'm going to sleep with you?"

"You heard my thoughts?" Santos went absolutely still as the truth began to ease into him. She had been thinking her questions to him, not speaking. And he'd heard every word. Clearly.

"Damn right I heard that." She wiggled beneath him, shoving, pushing until he shifted off of her to give her room to scoot out of the way.

She had heard his thoughts as he had heard hers. Worry niggled at him as he remembered a conversation he had had with a friend, another Guardian, Kieran MacIntyre, not so very long ago. Kieran had met a woman whose mind was not only open to him, but who could read his thoughts in return.

Santos remembered chuckling at his old friend's predicament—finding his Destined Mate. The Guardian legends spoke of Destined Mates. One woman meant for one man alone. The woman whose mind could mesh with his. The woman who was destined to be his throughout eternity.

Impossible.

"You should not have heard me," he said, easing away from her and wincing as the wound in his shoulder suddenly pulsed into aching life.

"Duh."

"Your psychic gift," he said, grasping for a straw. Any straw. "Does it also include telepathy?"

"No."

He sighed and stood up warily, still testing the air for danger. But the only danger here now was the threat to Santos's sanity. He was not a man meant for celibacy. In the centuries of his life, he had enjoyed countless women. With each, he had found and given pleasure freely, knowing that as an Immortal, he would not be staying with any of them for very long.

His world was made up of the hunt. Battles. The never-ending fight against the armies of darkness. This was the life he had chosen. The life he knew. He had no interest in a forever woman. His world was one of shadows and darkness. He had no time for light.

Always before, he slipped in and out of his lovers' minds, knowing what they wanted from him, what they needed, while keeping his own thoughts safely locked away.

Until tonight.

He looked at her and reached a hand out to her. "You heard my thoughts reflected in your mind?"

She ignored his offer of help and stood brushing off the seat of her jeans, and then the palms of her hands as she inched back from him, keeping her gaze locked on him as if she didn't trust him. *Him.* A man trusted by queens. A man who had spent centuries protecting the mortal world from the demon dimensions. Insulted, Santos glowered at her.

"Yes," she said, "I heard you. And I didn't come

here to be seduced. I came here for your help. If you can't give me that, I'll go."

"No. You will go nowhere," Santos said. "Not until I permit you to leave."

Chapter 5

Erin's heart was pounding so hard, she wouldn't have been surprised to see it batter its way past her rib cage and jump right out of her chest.

But it wasn't just the gunshot that had her standing so close to the edge. It was Santos himself. God. That kiss. That rush of sensation, as if her body was only now waking up to the potential of what it was meant to be. One touch from him and she was on fire. One kiss and her core was hot and needy and ready for him.

"Could my life get any weirder?"

"Come with me," he ordered and grabbed her hand.

When his fingers curled around hers, she felt a fresh new jolt of passion erupting within. Images— hot, sweaty *naked* images—raced through her brain.

"Don't touch me!" She tried to pull away, but he was much too strong to let her escape.

He flashed her a quelling look that probably worked on everyone else he knew. But Erin wasn't going to be cowed by this man. Not for a minute.

"Don't give me that look. I don't want you touching me. Not at all, okay?"

In answer, he bent low, tucked his left shoulder into her abdomen and stood, forcing her to hang upside down over his back.

"Put me down this minute," she shouted, slamming her fists into his spine until she remembered that he'd been shot and then she felt so damn guilty, she stopped. He'd been shot because of her. Wounded because he'd jumped in front of her, put himself in danger to save her. And she was screaming at him like *he* was the bad guy.

"Please," she said, her voice a tight strain of nerves and worry and fear. "Just let me down. When you touch me I see…"

He never stopped moving. He stalked into the

bedroom, across the floor and out into the hallway. His legs were long and he moved so quickly, so quietly, they were headed down the staircase before he answered.

"I know exactly what you see."

That got her attention. "You're reading my mind? *Now?*"

"Yes." One word, short and sweet.

Erin wanted to cringe. Her brain was filled with sexual images. *She and Santos, tangled together in bed, draped across each other. Her, bent over the side of the bed, he standing behind her, holding her in place as he took her...* "Oh, God."

"Do me the honor to stop thinking," he muttered at the bottom of the staircase. Then he shouted, "Thomas!"

From somewhere down the hall, another man called, "In the kitchen!"

Desperately, Erin tried to get her mind off of the images still taunting her, tormenting her. Multiplication tables! *Two times two is four. Two times three is six. Six. Sex. Sex with Santos. Sex in the bathtub. Sex by the fireplace. SEX.*

"Aaarrgh..."

"Well said," Santos muttered thickly.

He hit a swinging door hard and Erin pushed

herself up to look around a gigantic kitchen. Blue walls, white cabinets and stainless steel appliances ringed the cavernous room. The scent of roasting meat filled the air and fluorescent lights shone down from a high ceiling. The tiled floor was glistening in the overhead lights and sparkled back up at Erin as Santos swung her off his shoulder, dropped her to her feet and took a step back.

The couple at the table stood up and looked from her to Santos. He said, "Erin, this is Thomas and Amy Hawthorn. They work here."

They were both tall, but everyone looked tall to Erin. Thomas was lean and muscled and his wife was just as athletic looking. Her black hair was cut short and coaxed into tufty spikes all over her head. Though the man looked friendly enough, the woman's eyes narrowed as she looked at Santos.

"You're hurt," she said, almost like an accusation.

"It is nothing."

"He was shot," Erin blurted.

"Shot?" Amy hurried around the curve of the table and headed for Santos.

Thomas's eyes narrowed and his features tensed. "Who? Demon?"

"I don't know," Santos said shortly. "That's what I must look into."

"Let me see that wound," Amy said. "I'll get the kit and clean that out…"

"It's not necessary, thank you."

"Demon?" Erin asked, looking from one to the other of them until her gaze settled on Santos. "Did he say *demon?*"

Amy was tugging at Santos's bloodstained shirt. "You should at least let me clean it before it heals."

"It is almost closed already," he said, "I feel it." To Erin, he said, "You will stay inside the house with Thomas and Amy until I return."

"Return from where?" She curled her fingers around the edge of the blue granite countertop. "And what do you mean, demons?"

"This is not the time."

"What do you want me to do?" Thomas said, stepping in front of Erin to catch Santos's eye.

"Stay inside. The wards will keep demons out, but evil of the human kind may find a way past them."

"Right. And her?" He jerked his head to indicate Erin.

"Keep her safe." Santos sent her a long, thoughtful look. "Watch her."

"Just a damn minute," Erin said, pushing Thomas to one side, which wasn't easy since he didn't want to be moved. "I came to you for help."

"And got him shot," Amy snapped in a clipped, British accent. "Nicely done."

"I didn't shoot him," Erin argued, though right about now, she was thinking that might not be a bad idea.

Santos, realizing that arguing with Amy would only waste time, shrugged out of his bloody shirt and let her examine the wound. Erin had to fight to keep from batting the other woman's hands away from Santos's chest. God, he was gorgeous. Broad and muscled and brown.

Her heart twisted at the sight of the dried blood on his right shoulder, but amazingly enough, he had been right. His skin was smooth and unmarked. As if the bullet had never torn through his body at all.

"How?" she whispered, moving close and reaching out to touch his skin with the tips of her fingers.

He caught her hand in his, stopping her cold, then releasing her again to prevent their mental link. "It is a story for another time."

"I'll get another shirt," Amy said, sending Erin

yet another furious look. "While I'm gone, take a towel from the door, get that dried blood off of you."

Thomas rolled his eyes at his wife's bossiness, but Santos had learned in the scant three weeks he had known the couple that simply doing what Amy suggested was much easier than trying to argue with her. While Thomas talked about shutting down the house and keeping Erin safe, Santos took a dish towel and wet it at the sink.

"Let me do that," Erin said, taking the towel from him before he could fight her on it. "I don't understand what's going on. I mean…" She kept her voice low enough that Thomas couldn't hear them even if he had been listening. While she talked, she smoothed the damp cloth over his skin, wiping away the dried blood and marveling anew that his skin was already healed. Without a scar.

Shaking her head, she said, "I know what you are. Immortal. I saw that, *felt* that in my visions. But demons? You were talking about demons as if they really existed. What's going on? What more are you? What's happening that I don't know about?"

Santos turned his head and speared her with a dark gaze that demanded she heed him. Demanded her compliance and once again, she was forced to acknowledge that his gaze was very nearly hypnotic. She felt the power of that stare slide directly into the heart of her.

"You will wait here for me. You will not go outside. It is not safe." His voice brushed across her mind, the soft, firm tone both compelling and irritating. "When I return, we will talk."

"Why don't we talk now?" She stood back from him, tossed the stained towel into the stainless sink and shifted a look at Thomas. "You said yourself the danger was gone."

"I must make certain that no others are lying in wait."

"Here," Amy announced as she hurried back into the room. She held out a black, long sleeved shirt and Santos took it, slipping into it while he spoke to Thomas.

"Maintain the perimeter. Lock all entrances and keep her in the study. It is the easiest room to defend if it should come to that."

"Don't worry about a thing," Thomas assured him.

"I won't." He smiled briefly and gave the other man a nod of respect. "Remember, if the house is taken, there is the last room to retreat to."

"We know all that," Amy said, sliding a look at

Erin that was less than warm. "You do what you must. All will be well here."

"You're just going to leave?"

Santos turned to Erin and focused his gaze on hers. "I will return soon." He left the room with silent steps.

Thomas left a moment later to do a security check, which left Amy and Erin alone together. Erin felt the other woman's hostility and didn't even know how to combat it. But she had to say something.

"You're the reason he was shot, yes?" Amy asked before Erin could think of something friendly to say.

She wanted to deny the woman's words, but how could she? It was her the shooter had been after. She knew it. Felt it. "Yes, I guess I am," she said. "Someone's trying to kill me."

Amy nodded, wrapped her arms around her middle and looked at the door through which her husband had just disappeared. Then shifting her gaze back to Erin she said, "And now that someone is after us."

"Look," Erin said, "I didn't mean to bring this down on you guys, but—"

"It's here now, it will be handled."

Stung, Erin lifted her chin and said, "I'm not real thrilled with all of this, either, you know. If there was somewhere else I could go, I would. I just—"

"Stop." Amy shook her head, held up one hand, and then said, "You're right. This wasn't your choice and the fact that danger has appeared should be nothing new to me. It's only that danger from the human world is rare. But you've no reason to apologize. Honestly. It's not you I'm angry with. What's happened wasn't your fault. It's in Santos's nature to defend those who need help. He could no more go against the instinct to protect than he could stop breathing."

Erin was still stuck on Amy's use of the words "human world." "What exactly do you mean?"

"We're used to holding the house against evil," Amy said, her gaze worriedly shifting around the room, checking that the windows and doors were closed against the night outside. "But the human kind of threat is something new for us. Having it thrown at us without warning is…worrisome."

"*Human* threat?" Erin repeated, hoping to heaven she'd heard the other woman wrong. "That's the second time you've said that. What other kind than human *is* there?"

Amy blew out a breath, grabbed Erin's hand

and tugged her over to the fridge. "There's a lot to tell and not much time to tell it. Why don't I talk while we put together some supplies."

"Supplies?"

"We're going to be holing up in the study," Amy said with a shrug and a distracted smile. "And we'll probably be hungry before the night is over."

Santos moved through the darkness, becoming one with it, feeling the night wind slide across his skin, the familiar scents of the area filling his mind. He carried his sword, his fist tight around the antique silver hilt.

The weapon had been a part of him for hundreds of years. Moonlight glittered off the deadly blade as Santos slipped from shadow to shadow, searching for the clues he needed.

Demons he knew how to fight. Battle after battle stretched out behind him, one bleeding into another in his memories. But the human mind was more complex. More unpredictable.

And if there were humans behind Erin's troubles, Santos would have to call on not only his own vast knowledge, but that of his fellow Guardians. While he scanned the wide, sloping yard and the trees lining the edges of the property, his mind turned to thoughts of Erin. She was going to be difficult.

A part of him wished he could walk away from the problems she presented. But even as he considered it, he knew he couldn't. For whatever reason, she had come to him. Had known how to find him. That must mean something.

Laughing shortly, quietly, he called himself all kinds of a fool. It wasn't just the Fates leading Erin to him for protection. There was more. There was her taste. Her scent. The fact that their minds had linked. Though he didn't want to admit it, he knew there was a very real possibility that she was his Destined Mate. Whether he wanted her in his life or not, she was here now and he must find a way to both protect her from her enemies and keep her from becoming too important to himself.

He was caught in the web of a woman, as surely as the Guardian netting could trap a demon.

And that was simply unacceptable. He would help her. Defeat her attackers. See her safe.

Then he would see her on her way.

The whispered roar of the ocean sounded in the night like the heartbeat of a beast. The rise and fall of the waves against the shore pulsed in the very air, and Santos felt the power of it fill him.

He paused beneath the leafy shadows of an ancient oak and tasted the night scents, hoping to find...*there.* Faint, but true, the aroma of gunpowder still clung to the wind. He followed it carefully, watching his steps, though his nearest neighbor was more than an acre of land away. Not for the first time, he wished the Guardian house was more separate. More private. But the house had stood here, on the cliff, for more than a hundred years.

When it was new, it stood alone, a sentinel high above the sea. But as the years passed, more and more of the land was developed until the privacy a Guardian required was harder than ever to come by. Perhaps, Santos thought, that was part of the reason the last Guardian who had lived here had ended his existence.

It was hard enough to keep apart from humanity. But to live right alongside the very mortals you were sworn to defend and still be separate would be a difficult thing to contend with. Your very isolation would be that much more defined...knowing that others all around you belonged to the world in a way you never could.

"You are becoming maudlin, Santos," he murmured as he stopped beneath the branches of a massive maple tree. "It is enough. Do your job. Save the woman, *then* save yourself."

Sliding his sword into its scabbard, he swung himself up into the heavy branches of the maple tree and climbed quickly, following the lingering remains of the scent of gunpowder. Here, there was more. The cloying remnants of a musky after-shave, the sharp sting of tobacco.

Santos turned, sat on a branch and stared at the house. From this vantage point, the attacker had had a clear shot at the balcony off the master bedroom. In his mind's eye, Santos saw himself and Erin as they had been such a short time ago.

"We made it very easy for him," he mused and ground his back teeth together in a burst of fury that nearly choked him. She had come to him for protection and had nearly died in his home. The edges of his vision blurred with the rage coursing through him, making his blood churn, his heart-beat pound.

The threat to her would be dealt with. She would not be in danger again. "She is now under my protection and she *will* be safe. This I swear."

* * *

Erin helped Amy by setting out the sandwiches and bottles of water they'd carried into the study. She felt as though she were in an old Western movie. Hiding in a fort, hoping the Apaches wouldn't attack.

God. Apaches seemed like fluffy kittens after everything Amy had told her.

"Demons." She said the word aloud, testing it, trying to see if hearing it spoken somehow made it seem more plausible.

Nope.

Didn't help.

Thomas built a fire in a stone fireplace that made the one in the master bedroom look like a campfire ring. The hearth was big enough for Santos to stand in and when the fire caught, the blaze was high enough to signal ships at sea. But the heat helped. The snap and hiss of the flames helped. She was grateful for any sound that kept her mind too busy to think about Santos, out in the darkness, facing who knew what.

"He'll be fine, you know," Thomas offered from his seat across the room.

Erin glanced at him. "Please don't tell me you read minds, too."

"No," he said, smiling. "Just faces. I can see plainly that you're worried about him. But there's no need."

Worried? Was she worried about a man she'd only just met? Okay, *yes*. But surely that was understandable. She'd come to him for help. If something happened to him, Erin was on her own again. Not a happy thought.

"I told you," Amy said, patting her husband's knee as she curled up on the couch beside him. "Santos has been a warrior for centuries. He knows what he's doing."

"I still think you shouldn't have said anything," Thomas complained. "Santos won't be happy."

Amy shrugged and ran one hand over the spiky tufts of her hair. "He allowed her in here. Offered her his protection. And," she said, with a quick smile at Erin, "it's not like she didn't know some of it already."

"She's right," Erin said, rubbing her hands up and down her arms. She was cold again. The heat of the fire notwithstanding, there was an iciness in her blood that wouldn't go away. Well, no, that wasn't completely true, she thought wildly. She hadn't felt cold when Santos was kissing her, holding her.

Shaking her head, she smiled at Thomas. "You heard Santos. He was going to have a 'talk' with me when he gets back anyway. Now, he doesn't have to talk so much."

"Exactly," Amy said. "Besides, Erin is fine. She didn't panic. She's not hysterical."

Not on the outside, anyway. "I think that's because I'm having a really hard time believing all this," Erin said.

"A woman who can touch a bottle and see the man who last drank from it has trouble believing in the underworld." Thomas blew out a breath and reached for the shotgun at his knee. Leaning forward, he set it down on the wide coffee table in front of him. "Why is that?"

"Oh," Erin argued, still fighting to keep from shivering. "I believe in the underworld. And in a life beyond this one—I just had no idea that our world and those occasionally brushed up against each other."

She turned toward the heavy drapes covering the wide window that overlooked the front yard of the big house. She stared hard at them as if she could see through the fabric to the night beyond. "And knowing that Santos has spent his life fighting *demons*..."

"Successfully," Thomas added.

"Yes," she said, holding to that word. He was fine. He was doing what he was best at. What he had spent centuries doing. And yet, the cold at her core remained and the tension in her muscles strained her self-control. She wanted to know what he was doing. See that he was safe. And why did she care so much about a man she had known less than a day?

Because she needed his help to stay alive, of course. But even as she considered that reason, she knew it wasn't all there was to it. She cared what happened to Santos. More than she should.

More than she wanted to.

Shouts.

Erin lifted her head, spun around to look at Thomas and Amy, then back at the drapes. "Did you hear that?" she whispered. "I heard shouting. Right outside."

She started for the window before Thomas could stop her.

"Come away from the window!"

Throwing open the drapes, she looked down into the yard and her breath caught in her throat.

Santos.

Battling some...*thing*.

Santos howled and charged the gray, horned demon who had dared challenge him at the very gates of the Guardian home. It never would have breached the magical wards protecting the property if it hadn't attacked, attaching itself to Santos as they flew into the yard. They hit the ground hard, separating as they rolled across the damp grass. The demon's scent was thick and hot with the stench of sulfur. Its empty white eyes glittered weirdly in the moonlight and in one huge hand, it held a blade—more machete than sword.

Santos gained his feet, smiled at his opponent and felt the familiar swell of battle readiness sweep through him.

Sword high, he swung it at waist level and nearly cheered when the demon avoided that blow. He found that he needed a fight. Needed a battle that would clear his mind for the tasks ahead. Clear it of the rage still clouding his thoughts, and boiling his blood.

The demon shrieked, a haunting call at a pitch that should have cracked all the glass surrounding their fight. But Santos didn't care. He didn't worry about being seen by those outside the property. There were trees enough to provide a natural screen for the small war playing out under the moonlight.

"Guardian, you will pay."

"Demon, you've chosen the wrong night to challenge me. You will be returned to your hell, but I do not promise you will arrive there healthy." He leaped across the space separating them, turned in midair and swung the heavy sword in a deadly arc as he landed.

The demon shrieked again as the blade connected, severing one of its long, scaly arms. Santos smiled again, his eyes narrow, his features calm, sure.

Once again, swords clashed and howls of rage split the night. Santos gave the demon his attention and focused his rage on the capture of the beast that would dare challenge him on his home ground.

Again and again, the clash of metal against metal sounded out, sparks shot from the silver blades as though the fires of hell were locked within the heavy weapons.

Behind him, the house shone with light streaming from every window, laying down patchwork slices of gold on the lawn. Inside that house were three people who counted on him to do his duty. To keep them—and humanity—safe. And Santos felt that burden and lifted it eagerly.

This was where he belonged. This was who he was. Who he was always meant to be. A surge of power, complete, elemental, raced through him and with a final blow, he sent the demon to its knees. Santos finished it off with a hard kick to the chin. As it curled up on the grass, keening a high wail of pain and desperation, Santos felt someone watching him and turned to look up at the house.

His gaze caught Erin's, as she stood in the study window, watching him. He couldn't see her expression. And her mind was a racing jumble of thoughts, images, fears and doubts. No one stood out from the other. But he felt the power of her eyes on him and that, for the moment, was enough.

Chest heaving with exertion, Santos nodded at her, then swept her an elegant, courtly bow.

Chapter 6

"You fight demons."

"Yes."

"Actual demons."

Santos sighed and lifted a snifter of brandy for a long sip. After the battle on the lawn, he had returned the beast to its dimension and then come back to the house to face what appeared to be an endless stream of questions from Erin. "Yes. Actual demons. Do you doubt your own eyes?"

"No, but—"

"Amy should not have told you all of this."

"You're right," Erin said shortly. "*You* should have."

"There was hardly the time—" he paused and inclined his head "—nor, if you'll forgive me, the necessity."

"Huh! I think it's pretty darn necessary to know about *demons* wandering around town!" Stubborn, arrogant man. He wanted to keep his secrets while ferreting out hers. Well, she needed to know a few things. Way more than a few things.

Erin kept pacing. She'd been pacing for the last couple of hours. As if her body was racing to keep up with her mind. Even after Amy had explained to her about Guardians and demons and all of the other things, she really hadn't believed any of it.

Until she'd looked out the front window and seen that thing in battle with Santos.

"They do not wander. They come into this world for specific reasons."

Whirling around now to look at him from across the room, she asked, "And those are?"

He sipped at the amber-colored brandy, then held the glass up to admire the light filtering through the fine liquor. "Murder, mayhem. Sometimes thievery. Always trouble."

Right, because we didn't have nearly enough of

that stuff from the human variety of creep. "What did you do with it when you left here?"

He shrugged, a lazy movement of his shoulders that shifted the muscles of his chest in a way that made Erin's mouth go dry. Seriously, even when she was angry and scared, the man packed a hell of a punch.

"I returned it to its own dimension."

"Right. Demons not from this dimension. Sure. That makes sense." She nodded, half remembering Amy telling her something about portals and hell worlds and oh, God. She took a breath, blew it out and asked the question chewing at the back of her mind. "Is it a demon chasing me then? Is that why I never really see it? Only feel it watching me?"

He stood, set his brandy glass down on the coffee table and walked across the study to her. His strides were long, his movements so stealthy, a Navy SEAL could have taken lessons from him. He radiated danger. It pulsed out around him like a warning beacon and yet, Erin wasn't afraid. Not of him, anyway.

The way he made her feel? That was something else entirely.

Stopping in front of her, he reached out one

hand, then hesitated before actually touching her. She knew why. She knew he was trying to avoid the mental link between them. She could sense his reluctance to deepen it. Though his thoughts drifted through her mind, they were still individually hazy. But the overall sense of wariness came through loud and clear.

And she wasn't sure how she felt about that. Not that she wanted to read his mind or have him in hers, but the fact that he was deliberately trying to avoid it was unsettling.

Was he hiding something from her?

"It may be a demon behind the attacks on you," he said, his voice a low rumble of sound that danced across her nerve endings like a live wire. "But the one who shot at you was human."

"You're sure?"

One eyebrow lifted and a corner of his wide mouth tugged briefly. "Yes. I am sure. His scent lingered where he lay in wait."

"You could *smell* him?"

He nodded. "If he comes near the house again, I will be able to sense him in the area. Track him. Make him tell me why he is after you."

"Some consolation, I guess," she said and wrapped her arms around her middle in an unconscious attempt to ward off the cold seeping back into her system.

Once Santos had returned from wherever he'd taken the demon, Thomas and Amy had gone to bed, leaving Erin alone with the man she didn't know but was forced to trust. She'd seen him battle a demon, for heaven's sake. What was she supposed to think of that?

"Come," he said and this time, took her hand in his, drawing her over to the long, plush sofa near the fireplace. "You are cold again."

Her fingers trembled in his as visions raced through her mind. Hot, melty visions designed to batter away at the defenses she usually kept up between herself and oh, say, the rest of the world. She grabbed hold of him tightly, took a deep breath and closed her eyes, fighting off the rush of images.

"What do you see now when you touch me?" he asked.

Her eyes opened in an instant. "You're not reading my mind?"

"No. Our connection is not so close that we are linked completely. Before," he said softly, "I was caught unprepared. I did not expect a link to form when we kissed." He bowed his head in an Old

World gesture of respect. "And, I do not intrude uninvited."

"That's good," she whispered. She hadn't exactly liked the idea of him having an Anytime-You-Want-To Pass into her mind. Let's face it, some thoughts should remain private. She couldn't imagine living with a man who always knew what she was thinking.

"But if you are concerned, you can put up barriers against mental invasions."

"Yeah?" She followed him as he led her across the room and sat down on the sofa beside him. "How?"

"I will teach you. But for now, I ask again, what is it you are seeing now?" One dark eyebrow lifted. "Are these images the same as those you experienced earlier when we kissed?"

"No." Fine. She lied. Shoot her. But darned if she was going to tell him that yes, she was having lots more of the too sexy to be believed visions. She didn't want him getting the wrong idea about her. She hadn't come to him to play slap and tickle in that gigantic, soft, wonderful bed of his. She could hardly believe herself what she was feeling when he touched her. Not only did images never happen when she touched a person, but these X-rated images were just so unlike her.

She'd never been what she would have thought of as a totally sexual creature. Oh, she enjoyed the closeness of being with someone, but she didn't have all that much experience with *sex*. And the experiences she did have hadn't done much in the way of convincing her that all the romance novels had gotten it right.

There had never been fireworks. She'd never heard bells ring or seen pretty colors behind her eyes.

Which is why the visions of her and Santos in bed together were so confusing. In those images, she was completely abandoned, giving herself over to what felt like an ecstasy she had never known before.

But she wasn't about to tell him that.

"No?" he asked and one corner of his mouth lifted again. He didn't believe her.

"These are different," she said, letting go of his hand and smoothing her palms over her jeans. That wasn't a total lie. Along with the sexual images, there had been other pictures racing through her mind. "And they change and shift so quickly, I can't really acknowledge all of them."

"Tell me," he said, his dark gaze focused on her.

"I see you. Sometimes as you were on the ship."

He frowned in memory.

"Sometimes, I see you in a great hall," she said, her voice taking on a dreamy quality, as the memories crowded close, crushing out the present. "Like nowhere I've ever seen before. The walls are black, shining in a fiery orange light that shifts and dances like firelight. A crowd is there, but you're alone. And I know you're there, but I can't find you. I'm alone and there's screaming, wailing in the distance. It's so hot, I feel as though I'm burning up from the inside and I'm so afraid—"

Her voice broke off and she swallowed hard, slamming a mental door on the images that were too disturbing.

"This place you've seen does not seem familiar to me." When he spoke again, his voice was hushed, barely carrying over the hiss and crackle of the flames in the hearth. "You do not know where you are in this vision?"

"No." She shook her head and rubbed one hand across her eyes, as if that action could wipe away the images forever. "I've never seen any place like it. It feels…dark."

When she opened her eyes and looked up at him, she could have sworn for a moment his eyes were reflecting the weird, burning light she had seen in her mind. But then it was gone and his gaze was black and fathomless again as he watched her.

"These visions concern me."

"Me, too." Erin shivered again.

"You will stay here at this house," Santos said. "Until we discover what is behind these attempts on your life, you will remain. I will protect you. I will even help you uncover the truth."

"Thank you." Relief coursed through her on a wave so high and fast, she could scarcely breathe. She didn't know what she would have done if he had turned down her request for help. Go to the media as she had threatened? He had been right. No one would have believed her story.

"But know this," he added, his features stern, his gaze narrowed into slits, "I will not be tricked. Will not be played for a fool. If I find you are lying to me after all…"

She lifted her chin and met his gaze squarely. "I'm not."

"We shall see," he said, then picked up his brandy glass and leaned back into the sofa cushions. "Now. You will tell me all you know."

"Won't take long." She curled up on the couch and wrapped her arms around her knees. "As I said before, I never met my birth mother. I was adopted when I was an infant. My adoptive family is dead now, and as far as I knew, I was alone in the world until I got that letter from my birth mother."

"Five years ago."

"Yes." She could still remember the weird sensation of touching the cheap, floral stationery and knowing that the woman who had given her life had also touched it. "A law firm had been holding on to it until I turned twenty-five. They tracked me down in New York through my social security and employment records. After I read the letter, I contacted their offices, but they didn't know anything. The man who had originally agreed to hold the letter had long since retired, and no one at the firm had any further information."

"Where was this law firm?"

"Newport Beach."

"Here? In Southern California?"

"Yes." Erin leaned her head against the back of the couch. "I grew up there. When I left, I ran all the way to the east coast, but I guess Orange County will always be home."

"And then?"

She shrugged, as confused now as she had been at the time. "Then, nothing. I was scared, worried for a while, but nothing happened. There were no threats on me. No one was following me and nothing strange happened at all. Up until a few weeks ago, anyway."

"Which is when the danger erupted."

She sighed as the fire hissed and snapped behind her. Dancing flame shadows moved over the walls like writhing bodies. It felt as though she and Santos were alone in the world.

"Yes." She looked at him, staring directly into those shining black eyes and felt herself reaching instinctively for his strength. She'd been taking care of herself for so long, it was second nature to her. But Erin had finally come across something she couldn't handle on her own.

That was both terrifying and infuriating. She didn't want to *need* someone. Didn't want to have to be grateful to anyone for her mere survival. She wanted to run her own life and be beholden to no one.

But those days were gone now and she knew it.

Until this threat was resolved, her life hung in the balance.

"I turn thirty in three weeks. And it's pretty obvious that somebody somewhere doesn't want that to happen."

Santos frowned, reached for the old letter she'd dropped on the coffee table and read it aloud. "'My dear daughter. Though I have never held you in my arms, my love for you has never wavered. I send this letter as a warning. On your thirtieth birthday, your biological father is going to come for you. He will drain your psychic abilities and then kill you. You must be prepared. You must protect yourself as I have tried to, by giving you over to others to raise. Know that I will always love you. Your mother, Breanna Shea.'"

Erin shivered, rested her chin on top of her knees and waited for him to speak. When he did, she took no comfort from what he said.

"Your mother says that your father will kill you *on* your thirtieth birthday."

"Yes."

He looked at her and she felt the power of his stare right down to her bones. Just for a moment, she wished she *could* read what was in his mind right then. She tried, but only reached a blur of impressions, nothing solid. Nothing reassuring.

"What is happening to you," he said quietly, "suggests that there is someone else after you, as well. If your father is going to wait for your birthday to strike—who is after you *now?*"

* * *

But the answers would not be found that easily. So the next night, Santos took up his sword and went hunting. His duty must prevail over all things. It had been that way for hundreds of years. He couldn't allow even Erin and the dangers she faced to keep him from performing the obligation he owed the mortal world.

He followed the faint trace energy patterns staining the night air with wisps of color, like a memory of a rainbow. In the shadowy world he inhabited, those colors were all that had mattered to him in centuries. He lived and hunted and that was all. Life had become the hunt. Without it, Santos would be lost.

He stalked his prey through the old Presidio. People wandered through the well-lit areas. Couples mostly, they moved hand in hand, laughing, talking, pausing for a kiss among the shadows.

Santos noticed them, but instead of disregarding them all as he usually would, he found himself sparing them a thought or two. What secrets did they carry? What fears? What problems ruled their lives? Was their laughter a façade behind which to hide from reality? Did they wonder about the world around them? Or did they lose themselves in each other?

"Fool. What does it matter?" It had been hundreds of years since last Santos felt anything beyond lust for a woman. And that woman had betrayed his trust. Offered him up as a sacrifice to save her own beautiful neck. And so he'd met his death on the *Niña,* swallowed by the cold sea, only to be born again into a life he could never have imagined.

He had loved, then. He had looked at her and seen all of the beauty and power in the world. He'd given her his trust, his protection and laid his life into her hands, and he had paid the ultimate price for choosing his love poorly.

Now another woman had entered his life. One who wanted his trust. One who needed his protection as much as the other had. Dare he choose to help again? Dare he risk allowing her into his world?

Yet how could he not and call himself a Guardian? A defender of the innocent?

He scowled, irritated at himself for indulging in thoughts that had no place on a hunt. Refocusing his concentration, he sniffed the air and peered into the cover of darkness, searching for the energy patterns that would reveal the presence of the demon he sought.

Already, this demon had made itself known. Santos had trailed it from the beach where it had escaped the portal. The demon had killed once already—a young man, no more than a boy, really, who would never again sneak off into the night for a moonlight swim.

A scream shattered the night and Santos whirled in the direction of the sound. His gaze, as clear in the night as in the light of day, swept the area.

Presidio Hill was locked in darkness, only a pale light shone on the Padre Cross, built of tiles from the old Presidio. Palms and cypress surrounded the cross, giving it a look of a well-tended graveyard. The ghosts of the Presidio were thick here, the air always alive with their spirits, unwilling to leave the place that had once been such a thriving spot in what was then Alta California, under Spanish rule.

"We should have kept it," Santos told himself as he scanned the shadow filled darkness, searching for the enemy.

To the left was the Serra Museum and beyond that Palm Canyon and Inspiration Point. But Santos was focused on the Padre Cross. Moving quickly, he ran the length of the hill, swirling one hand around him to create a cloak that would keep him invisible to the eyes of humans.

Drawing his sword as he ran, he heard the strangled whimper of a woman and followed that distress-filled sound. He found a demon, crouched over the injured body of a man, while a woman backed against a ragged palm, trying to disappear.

"Enough!" Santos shouted and the demon responded in the blink of an eye. It whipped its head up, flame-red eyes fastened on Santos, and instantly left the human it had already desperately injured.

"Guardian," it muttered, voice rattling with the hatred that choked it. "You will not stop me. You cannot stop me."

"I can and I will," Santos promised, dismissing the two humans as he swiped his sword through the air, the blade whistling with deadly intent.

The demon charged, fangs bared, eyes blazing, clawed hands outstretched. Racing forward, it flew beneath the edge of the blade to lash out at Santos. He felt the slice of the claw as it raked across his midsection, but he ignored the pain, focusing only on the battle. Swinging wide, Santos held his sword aloft and brought it down in a fierce arc, catching the demon across its spine.

A howl rent the air, the sound scraping across Santos's mind like a spike driven hard and deep. Springing up again, the demon faced him in the wavering light of the moon and spat words in a torrent of vitriol.

"You battle me, Guardian, while the woman dies?"

Santos spun his head for a quick look. The woman was crouched over her fallen lover, cell phone in her hand, calling for help. She'd lost sight of her attacker, as the demon, too, was hidden by the cloak of the Guardian.

"The woman lives," Santos said. "And will continue to do so as you, my scaled friend, will soon be back in your own dimension."

"Not that pitiful human." A wide, vicious mouth opened in mocking laughter as the demon dropped to a crouch, peering up at Santos through narrowed eyes, still flaring with the flames of hell. Moonlight pooled around it as a shining spotlight.

"I speak of the woman who ran to you for protection, Guardian. *She* is the one who dies tonight. Unless you prevent it, there are those who will kill her to avert her destiny."

Santos felt a chill. A demon would lie to protect its own hide and there had been many over the ages who had tried and failed to bargain with him for their freedom. But the taunts of this demon rang true. It had nothing to gain but the pleasure of seeing Santos falter.

Instantly, he turned his face into the ever-present wind and reached out with his mind, trying to link with Erin. But there was nothing. No connection. As if the tie between them had been severed. He had been so careful to keep a mental distance from the woman—and now that he needed to reach her, he couldn't.

He had no time to waste on a prolonged battle. Swiftly, Santos lunged, driving the tip of his sword into the narrow, concave chest of the demon before him. He had no qualms about doing whatever he had to do to get this demon to talk. If they were in the demon's dimension, this wound would have been fatal. But not here. Here, it could only be an impetus to talk.

With the beast impaled, Santos looked down at it dispassionately. "Speak," he demanded. "Speak now before I give you more pain to carry with you to your own hell."

It arched up, inadvertently driving the sword even deeper into its own flesh. The pain would be hideous, but the demon wouldn't die of its wound.

Demons were almost impossible to kill in this dimension. The most a Guardian could hope for was to wound it severely enough to hasten a fast trip back to its own world. There, it would heal and regenerate until it inevitably planned another escape into *this* world.

The only thing that could kill a demon on the human plane was "the blood of the innocent." Santos had never been sure what that meant until he had learned of Kieran MacIntyre's Mate, offering her own life to save Kieran's in a battle with a demon. Her blood, freely given, had spilled across the demon, destroying it utterly.

Grabbing hold of the blade with long-fingered, clawed hands, the demon screeched again, spitting at Santos with hate-filled eyes. "She dies. Our kind and hers both want her. One will have her." It tugged ineffectively at the blade driven into its chest. "You cannot save her, Guardian. Her time in your world is over."

Black, undiluted rage throbbed inside Santos like another heartbeat as the demon's words repeated over and over again in his mind. Demons and humans alike wanted her dead?

Who was Erin? What reason could so many have for wanting her death? Why did the thought of her ending cause a black spill of emptiness to slide through him?

And *why* did she not respond to his call?

His mind reached for her again and again, demanding she answer. There was nothing.

With the demon's maniacal laughter ringing out around him, Santos bundled it into the Guardian net. Then leaving it, contained and invisible to the mortal world, Santos raced back down the hill to his car.

He had to get back to the Guardian house. He had to find Erin. If the demon was telling the truth, she needed him.

Now.

And for the first time in centuries, he felt powerless.

Chapter 7

"It will be so much easier this way, dear."

Erin's head pounded and her vision blurred, colors swirling together. Music filled the air, soaring, weeping, strings and horns pulsing with a life all its own. Sights and sounds melded into one cacophonous roar that swelled by the second. Overpowering, overwhelming, her surroundings became a carnival ride of regret and fear.

Something was wrong. The study. She knew she was in the study at Santos's house. But nothing looked as it should. Nothing *felt* as it should.

She tried to lift one hand to rub her forehead,

but couldn't seem to make her arm cooperate. That wasn't right. Why couldn't she move? Why couldn't she see? It was as if she were…*absent.* As if she'd already left her body and was even now hovering overhead, staring down at a scene that shouldn't…couldn't, be happening.

A familiar face swam in front of Erin and she knew she should recognize the woman. She tried. She really tried. Blinking, staring, shaking her head to try to clear the blurriness. Focus, Erin, focus.

The woman's face faded in and out, smearing at the edges. Red-lipsticked mouth smiling, empty blue eyes flat, unemotional. An older woman with violet-tinged hair sprayed into an unmovable helmet on her head. *Familiar.* A woman who wore pink as her signature color and had sneakers in every color of the rainbow.

"Maggie?" Erin whispered as her head flopped against the back of the couch.

"Yes, dear, it's Maggie," the older woman soothed, her voice slow, careful, calming. "I've come to take care of everything. You shouldn't have run, you know, dear. It only makes it harder on you."

Erin tried to think, willed clarity into her mind

and was only marginally disappointed when it didn't happen. Something. She should be doing something. Saying something. But she was tired. So tired. Couldn't hold her eyes open anymore.

"Thomas?" she whispered, knowing somehow that the man who worked for Santos was here in the house somewhere. He would know what to do. He could send for Santos. For the big Guardian who would keep her safe. Santos would be here. Soon, Thomas would call him.

Why couldn't *she* call Santos?

She reached for the Guardian with her mind, but it was a muddle of nonsense. She couldn't make sense of her own thoughts, let alone reach for someone else's.

"Oh, now dear, Thomas and Amy won't be a problem." The kind, quiet voice spoke to her from close by and Erin knew she should open her eyes, look at the woman. Why couldn't she open her eyes?

"I've taken care of them," Maggie said, a pleased note in her voice now. "A little something in the tea, you know. It's better this way."

"Tea…" That's right, Erin thought wildly, fighting for coherency, fighting to regain the thoughts she'd lost. She'd had tea with Maggie

Shannon. An old friend of her adoptive mother's. How had the woman come to Santos's house? Oh, yes, Erin nodded, smiling as the memory came to her. Good. A good sign. She was thinking again.

She had called Maggie. Asked her to come to San Diego. She'd hoped that Maggie would know something. That perhaps Erin's adoptive mother had told her best friend something that could help Erin discover who and what was after her.

They'd had tea in the study. Lovely room. A fire in the hearth. Music on the CD player. Santos gone. Off fighting something. Thomas and Amy here. Everything safe. Good. Everything okay.

Her heart skittered unevenly in her chest, pumping hard and fast as fear reasserted itself and shot adrenaline through her body. Fear. Of Maggie. Yes. Something wrong. Something desperately wrong.

"No," Erin said, lifting her head with an enormous strength of will. Her eyes opened into tired slits and watched the old woman she'd known most of her life. But this Maggie was a stranger. Her eyes were blank. Her lipsticked mouth set in a grim line of disapproval.

"Now, now, no sense in fighting this, Erin dear. It's not a strong drug, but it will make you very sleepy. And that's as it should be. Just let me do what I must and it will all be over. Poor little thing, frightened to death. That shouldn't have happened, really. But you brought this on yourself." Maggie sighed and patted her immovable hair. "Coming to a Guardian for help. Really, dear, that's simply not done. Certainly not by someone like *you.*"

"Guardian?" Erin whispered the word, thinking she was shouting. "You know? About Santos?"

"Of course I do, dear. Why," she said, smiling widely now, "we know all there is to know. We make it our business. Now you just lie back and relax. Trust me that I'm doing what's best for you. For all of us."

Maggie pulled a dagger from the depths of her purse and Erin gasped, fear erupting inside her anew in a thick, hot wave that threatened to choke her. She should run. She should get up off the couch and race from the room. She had to hide. Had to get away.

But she couldn't move.

The dagger looked old—the blade was shining silver and the hilt was covered in an intricate design of interlinked swirls of silver on black. Whispering words that floated through Erin's mind and disappeared, Maggie cupped the blade on her open palms and bowed her head before lifting her gaze to Erin again.

Inching back on the sofa, trying to drag her leaden body away from the woman she had loved, Erin croaked out a single word. "Why?"

"For humanity, of course." Maggie's pale blue eyes suddenly sparked with the light of a zealot. Her fingertips caressed the blade and turned it so that the firelight caught on the shining silver and winked with danger. "You must end, Erin. Before your birthday."

Oh, God. Her throat tightened, her still-spinning mind tried to veer away from what was happening, but fear roared up and asserted itself.

"No, no, Maggie, don't…" She shook her head and the room tilted wildly, furniture climbing walls, ceiling lights dancing on the floor. Her stomach lurched and she fought for air. For strength.

Maggie stood, clutching the dagger in one tight fist. She smoothed her free hand down the front of her pink velour sweater, pausing briefly over the appliquéd white poodle. "I am sorry, dear, I do wish there were another way, but there's really no choice."

She took a step and her sneakers squeaked slightly on the hardwood floor.

"Maggie, please…"

Clucking her tongue, the older woman shook her head in disapproval. "It's time, Erin. And after all, you really shouldn't be so greedy, dear. It isn't seemly. You've had thirty years of life, you know. Thirty wonderful years. And I allowed that. I *fought* for you. I wanted you to live as long as you could. Experience all that life could afford you—before, of course, the inevitable end."

"You let me live?" None of this made sense. Erin had the feeling that even if her head were clear, none of it would make sense.

"Of course I did. There were others, you see," Maggie was saying and now she sighed. "I must tell you, *they* wanted you to die when you were only a child. They felt that taking care of the threat then would ensure the world's safety. But I fought for you," she said, smiling and nodding as if she expected gratitude instead of fear.

Who were these others Maggie was talking about? People who had watched Erin her whole life? People who held the power of life and death over her?

"I insisted that you be allowed to live as long as you could," Maggie said, lovingly stroking one finger along the antique blade. "So see, dear?

You've already had more of life than some wanted you to have. Don't feel badly. It won't hurt. I promise."

"You protected me from those…*others?*" Erin fought for clarity, knowing it was the only way she could survive this. Knowing that she had to keep Maggie talking. Keep her from using that dagger. Knowing that she *had* to survive until Santos came. She tried to reach him telepathically, but there was only the blur and haze of a mind befuddled by the drugs Maggie had given her.

"Yes, dear. I've watched over you always." Maggie smiled again and took a seat on the sofa. "It was my assignment. Since I had argued for your prolonged life, I was told to get close to you. But naturally, I came to care for you. Believe me when I say this is most difficult for me."

Difficult for *her?*

Hysteria rose up inside her and she clamped her mouth shut to keep the wild laughter from escaping.

Maggie was close, Erin thought. Too close. She tried to scoot back farther, but her body wouldn't cooperate. Her arms were heavy. Her body felt as though it had melted into the sofa.

"Try to relax now, dear."

"What?" Erin's throat tightened and tears filled

her eyes, then spilled over to rain unchecked down her cheeks. "Relax?" She blinked, focused and asked, "What're you doing? Maggie?"

God. Let me think. Let me move. Let me do *something* besides lay here and wait for death.

Maggie patted her hand and Erin wanted to flinch away from her, but still, she couldn't move.

"I'm very good at this, dear. I do promise it won't hurt." Maggie leaned in closer, still smiling, holding out the dagger as she moved. "One quick swipe and it will all be over."

The room exploded in a shower of glass. Santos leaped through the wide front window and landed, legs wide spread, arms outstretched, one hand grasping the hilt of a wicked sword. His dark eyes flashed and his howl of fury rattled the walls.

Maggie spun to face him, the quiet, tender old woman gone completely now, swallowed up by a madness that crouched in her eyes and spat from her mouth.

"You won't stop this, Guardian."

Erin sighed, relief flooding her system. Her head turned on the cushion and her gaze locked on Santos. He looked exactly what he was. An ancient warrior.

His black hair was loose, flying about his shoulders in wind streaming through the shattered window. His black shirt clung to his broad chest, gaping over his abdomen where the fabric had been sliced. His black leather pants were tucked into black boots and his dark eyes flashed with the light of battle. He swiped the blade through the air with a sharp action that made the metal sing. "Move away from her."

"No." The old woman's voice grated. "She dies. For the good of us all, she dies. Tonight." Whipping back around, Maggie lunged toward Erin.

Erin groaned and braced for the slice of the dagger across her throat.

Santos had only a moment. Instincts took over. He tossed his sword high, caught it like a spear and hurled it across the room.

"Aaaaahhhh!" Maggie shrieked, grabbed the end of Santos's sword protruding from her chest and staggered back one step. Two. Stunned, she looked down at Erin, then turned her head to stare dumbfounded at Santos. She fell then, tumbling across the coffee table and rolling over it to land on the floor. Curled up on her side, the long, lethal blade speared through her body, Maggie only whimpered.

Santos went first to Erin. His hands cupped her face, slid down her body, assuring himself that she was safe. He had driven his black BMW convertible like a madman. Weaving in and out of traffic, he'd raced back to the house, consumed by the blind fury the demon had sparked within him. Arriving at the house, he'd immediately sensed danger within, but finding an elderly woman with a dagger had been a surprise.

Relief coursed through him like a raging river. He hadn't arrived too late. He stared into Erin's eyes and saw that she was unhurt, but drugged. This, then, was why he hadn't been able to reach her mind no matter how desperately he'd tried.

Erin, his mind reached for hers and found only jumbled fears and terror. *You are safe. I will keep you safe. Sleep now.*

"You came," she whispered.

"I came. Now, be still." He left her then, leaping over the upset coffee table to land on the floor beside the dying old woman.

She glared at him as blood bubbled between her lips, frothing as she tried to speak, to curse him.

"Who sent you here?" he demanded, going down on one knee and staring hard into her eyes.

She coughed, groaned and forced a smile that never reached her eyes. "You have stopped me, Guardian. But others will come."

"Why?" He leaned in, using the strength of his

voice to reach her even as she was sliding away from this world and into the next. "Tell me why."

Her blue eyes closed, then opened again, focusing on him with an intensity that was surprising as she traveled so close to death. "If her father… cannot be stopped…she must die. Before he can…use her on her birthday. We are many," she warned, voice fading into a strangled whisper. "You cannot stop us all."

She died, her last breath sighing from her body and Santos turned from her, dismissing the would-be assassin. Going to Erin, he scooped her up off the couch and held her close, his arms folding around her.

Her head fell back and her eyes opened. Staring up at him, she weakly lifted one hand, touched his cheek, then let her hand drop again. "Thank you."

How had she come so close to death? Here, in what should have been a sanctuary?

Rage bubbled up inside him fresh and thick, but was tempered by the incredible relief of knowing she was safe again. For the moment. Glancing at the body on the floor though, Santos knew the danger wasn't over. The demon he'd trapped at the Presidio had said that both demons and mortals wanted Erin dead. This one old woman seemed to prove that statement true.

But why?

What did Erin possess that made her such a threat to both worlds? He looked down into her face and saw only a woman. A beautiful woman, confused and frightened and everything in him urged him to protect her. Defend her. No matter the cost.

He stalked from the room, unmindful now of the shattered glass or the body, lying on the floor behind him. He hit the foyer and headed for the staircase, but Erin roused herself, whispering, "Thomas. Amy."

He gritted his teeth and felt a surge of anger both at the intruder in his home and himself. He hadn't even thought to check on Thomas and his wife. His only thought had been for Erin. Getting to her. Protecting her.

But he knew already that something had happened to the couple. They would have been with Erin. Thomas would have done his best to protect her. Amy would have used her skills in defense. And if all else failed, Thomas would have sent both Erin and Amy into the panic room off the study. Since he had not, Santos could only assume that the man was either dead or, like Erin, drugged.

"I will see to them when you are cared for," he vowed. And with that promise, another one rose to the surface of his mind. This vow he took silently, and swore to it by all he held holy. He would find those responsible for the attack on his house. And when he did, they would never present a danger again.

He took the stairs two at a time, listening to the muffled thud of his own footsteps pounding like an erratic heartbeat. Striding into the master bedroom, he laid Erin down on the bed, then quickly checked her pulse. Steady. He took a breath and allowed himself a smile. Her heartbeat was strong. She would survive. And that was all that mattered. Covering her with a quilt he dragged up from the end of the bed, he went back down-stairs to check on the other mortals under his pro-tection.

"No. No, don't. Don't, Maggie. Please, don't do this…"

Erin's voice, soft, terrified, tore Santos from sleep. Instantly alert, he reached for the woman lying beside him on the wide bed. He pulled her into his arms and held her close, running one hand up and down her back in long, soothing strokes.

Tempted to reach into her mind, to read her thoughts, Santos resisted, giving her the privacy she no doubt needed. She had been sleeping for several hours and he was only thankful that she was awake again. "It is all right, Erin. You are safe. Maggie is gone."

He didn't need to tell her that Maggie's body had been left in an alley in downtown San Diego. She would be thought to have been a victim of random violence. There would be no link between the old woman and this house. He had taken her car and driven it to the bus station, wiping it clean of all trace of him. It was, except to Erin, as if Maggie had never come to this house.

Erin twisted in his grasp, her mind dealing with awakened memories, and when she gasped and yanked herself free of him, he let her go. Pushing both hands through her hair, she sat up on the bed and looked around wildly as if trying to understand where she was. What had happened.

"Santos." His name was a plea. A whispered call from her heart.

"I am here," he said and half turned to flick on the lamp on the bedside table. Instantly, pale yellow light shone in the darkness.

She closed her eyes. "No light. Please. No light."

"It is done." The lamp was snapped off a heart-beat later.

Shadows crept through the room, fed by moon-light that was a pale, silvery wash of color. Erin's dark red hair shone with a richness that took Santos's breath away. Her soft skin was porcelain fine, her eyes emerald pools of wounded hurt and confusion.

And she touched something in him Santos hadn't even been aware existed.

"Thomas?" she asked. "Amy?"

"Well." He drew one knee up and rested his forearm across it as he watched her. "They took less of the drug than you did. They woke two hours ago, furious, but unhurt. The drug was not a strong one. Meant only to incapacitate, not kill."

"No," Erin said, rubbing her eyes with the tips of her fingers. "You're right. She was going to use the dagger for that. She tried—she tried—" She lifted her head, her gaze spearing into his and he felt a punch of need so raw, so fierce, it took his breath.

He used all of his immense strength to remain still. She was vulnerable, frightened. And under his protection. He would not allow his own desires to rage uncontrolled when she was so very fragile. His hands fisted to keep from reaching for her.

More than simple desire, this new, unexpected sensation clamored at him to comfort, to care for, to ease Erin's pain.

"I don't understand," she whispered brokenly, shaking her head, allowing tears to fall, sliding down her cheeks in moonlit trails. "I invited her here because I wanted to ask her to help me. She was my mother's friend. She was *my* friend." She slapped one hand to her chest. "How could she do that to me?"

"She was not what you thought she was," Santos whispered, his voice a harsh whisper.

"Then who was she? Who am *I?*"

"We will find out, Erin. Together."

"And then?" Her voice cracked as she lifted one hand to her mouth. "When we find out the truth, what will I do then? What if I can't bear who I am? What if I find out I should *let* them kill me?"

"No." One word. Strong. Sure. "They will not kill you. You will not even begin to think that they should. What they are is of no consequence."

"Maybe there's something evil in me. Maybe that's why they want me dead. I don't know…" She shook her head and that rich fall of hair moved around her shoulders in a gentle dance of fire and light.

"I do." He reached for her, again following instincts that wouldn't allow him anything else. Gathering her close, he drew her onto his lap, cuddling her against his chest, whispering soothing nonsense as she fisted her hands in his shirt.

"You are not evil," he said, his voice soft, caressing.

"You can't be sure of that, Santos." She buried her face against his chest.

"I have battled evil for more than five hundred years," he said and his voice was soft now, convincing, hypnotizing. "I can feel it in the air when it is near. I sense its presence above all things."

Fires spread through his bloodstream as he tipped her chin up with his fingertips and stared into the eyes that held so much emotion, so much power.

"There is no evil in you, Erin. We will discover the truth," he vowed. "Together. I will not allow you to be hurt."

She turned her head to glance at the open French doors through which a chill wind blew, lifting the sheer draperies into an eerie, silent dance. "Are we safe here now?"

"Yes," he said, gritting his teeth. It infuriated him that she *hadn't* been safe. "Measures have been taken."

"Like…?"

He gave her a small smile. "The magical wards on the property have been strengthened."

"Wards?"

"Think of them as magical locks. Barred doors. They are normally set to keep out demons and allow mortals passage. As of tonight, they will repel mortals, as well. No one comes onto this property without my permission."

She blinked at him. "You can do that? Magic, I mean?"

"No, *querida*," he said, smiling. "Amy has done it."

"Amy?"

He lifted one shoulder in a careless shrug that belied the tension in his body. "She is a hereditary High Witch. Very powerful. Which is another reason she is so angry at the moment. She feels that she should have been aware of the old woman's intent."

"It's not her fault," Erin said softly.

"No," he agreed. "It is mine." She shook her head, but he discounted that motion and kept talking. "You are here. In my home. Under my protection. This should never have happened. And it will not happen again. I want you to know…to believe you are safe with me."

"I do." She took a deep breath, released it and said, "I'm the one who invited her here."

Instantly, he stiffened. "You will not do that again, Erin. Your safety is paramount. There will be no one else entering this house until we have resolved this."

"No problem," she said, huffing out another breath. "I don't think I want to talk to anyone." She pushed one hand through her hair, shoving it back and away from her face. "Maggie Shannon tried to kill me. If I can't trust her, then I can't trust anyone."

He sighed. "You may trust in me, Erin. I will not fail you again."

"You didn't fail me, Santos. You *saved* me."

He smiled and smoothed away a tear with the pad of his thumb. "Ricardo," he said. "Call me Ricardo."

She turned her face into his touch and closed her eyes on a sigh. "Ricardo," she repeated softly, catching her hand in his, holding it to her face as she looked up and fixed her gaze on his.

Slowly, he pulled her in closer, closer, until their mouths were only a breath apart. And when he could stand the suspense no longer, he lowered his mouth to hers. Hungry for another taste of her, Santos claimed what he knew to be his. Claimed the one woman who could reach inside him and find the heart he had long thought to be encased in ice.

One touch of her mouth and he was on fire. He needed. He hungered. In one swift move, he shifted, laying her on the bed and covering her with his own body. She lifted her arms, encircling them around his neck, holding him closer, tighter to her.

Her mouth opened for him and his tongue swept inside to taste her hidden depths. To devour. To take all she was into himself. It was as if she had been made for him. Every curve of her lush body aligned itself with his body as if she were the missing piece in the jigsaw puzzle of his life. He touched her and found fire. Tasted her and found life.

Ricardo...

He smiled against her mouth and answered her as she had spoken to him, mind to mind.

I must have you, Erin. Feel my need for you. See it in my mind.

Her mind opened to his and Santos was overcome with her thoughts pouring across his. Images, visions, rich with color and sound, filled him. Images of the two of them, together, locked in each other's arms. Pictures of her life before this. Her world as she had known it before it imploded around her.

He saw it all.

Saw her.

All of her. In one heart-stopping instant, he knew her better than he had ever known anyone in his too-long life.

I need you, too, Ricardo. Now. Please, now.

He deepened the kiss, giving her everything he had, everything he had ever been. He knew as her mind touched his more fully, that she was seeing his past, the long years of duty. Of loneliness. Of pain. He would have spared her if he could, but there was no hiding any of it from the woman who could touch him so deeply.

Tearing his mouth from hers, Santos stared down into those emerald depths and saw the stunned shock he was feeling mirrored there before him.

"Oh, my God." Erin's voice was harsh, strained with the need still pulsing between them. She looked up into his eyes and Santos felt the overwhelming sensations rocking her.

"I saw—"

"I know," he said, sweeping one hand up and down the length of her, over her abdomen, up to the curve of her breast.

She hissed in a breath, arching into his hand, her eyes sliding closed on a fresh burst of desire. Shaking her head on the silk duvet, she whispered, "I saw you. All those years. I saw...*you*."

"Open your eyes, *querida*," he said, his voice a deep, rich caress as complete as a touch. "Open your eyes and see me now."

She did, looking up at him with wonder in her eyes and Santos expelled a breath.

He was lost.

Chapter 8

She *did* see him.

Erin stared up into Santos's dark, deep eyes and felt herself falling into their depths. His features were tight, drawn with want, desire, and as she watched him, those dark eyes flashed silver and signaled his need to her.

His thoughts filled her mind and her body turned to liquid fire at the erotic images he showed her. Sighing, she reached up and framed his face with her palms, brushing his thick, black hair back with her fingertips. He was a pirate, a thief of hearts and souls, and she knew that another kiss from him would seal her fate. She would be completely lost inside him and she didn't care.

More than that, really.

She *wanted* it. Wanted to be so deeply embedded inside him she would never find her way out. Her whole life, she'd longed for this very feeling. To become a part of someone. Her adoptive parents had tried to give her a good life—until it had all fallen apart due to her "gift." But even before that night, she'd always felt a little like an outsider. Like she didn't really have a place in that house or in their lives. She'd always craved, more than anything else, to know that she had found somewhere where she was wanted, needed.

And the fact that she had found that comfort in the arms of the man she had run to for help seemed somehow…fated. As if she'd been brought here. To this house. To this man.

Lifting her head from the soft, feather pillow, she laid her mouth over his. He held perfectly still for several long seconds as she tasted him, teased him, parted his lips with her tongue. And then it was as if a cord binding him in place had suddenly snapped.

He was fire and lightning and earthquakes. The world rocked again as it had hours ago, only this time, she welcomed it. His body melded to hers.

His hands scraped beneath her clothing, sliding over her skin, igniting tiny infernos with every touch. Erin's breath caught as she arched into him, wanting more, needing more.

Instinctively, her mind reached for his. *Ricardo, I need you.*

His thoughts came in Spanish, his first language, his natural inclination.

Mi amor, debo tenerle ahora.

I don't understand, she answered, her body responding to the emotion underscoring the words she couldn't comprehend.

Erin felt him smile against her mouth, despite the firestorm of sensations flooding them.

Now, my love. I must have you now.

Good, good. Now would be wonderful.

Then all thought stopped. All attempts at communication faded as Erin gave herself up to Santos's gentle, thorough ministrations. Deftly, in less time than it took to think about it, he had her out of her clothes and stretched out naked against the cool blue silk duvet. The slide of the fabric against her bare skin felt sensual, wicked and she moved on it languidly, feeding her own sensual needs *and* that flash of inner fire in Santos's silver eyes.

He looked at her and she went up in flames. He touched her and her body exploded. He kissed her and she surrendered to the inevitable. He was all. He was everything. As he stood and stripped out of his clothes, Erin watched his every movement. Moonlight gilded his magnificent body, making it seem as though he were a statue of some ancient god, captured forever in tones of amber.

Then her eyes narrowed on a faint, red line stretching across his flat abdomen. "You're hurt."

He glanced down, then looked at her and smiled. "No, it is nearly healed already. The demon I fought tonight."

"Healed." Her gaze went to his shoulder where a bullet meant for her had torn through his body. But his skin was smooth, unmarred. "Amazing."

He shook his head, his long black hair falling about his face like a thick, silk curtain. "No, *querida,* you are the amazing one."

Erin sucked in a breath and let her gaze wander over him again. His hard, thick body was ready for her and she felt her insides quiver in expectation. She wanted him more than she had ever wanted anything else in her life. Lifting her arms to him, she arched her back off the bed, reaching for him, silently demanding that he come to her, take her, ease the want within.

Instantly, his dark eyes fired and he became a tortured, ferociously hungry male who looked at her as though she were his last meal. Erin's blood quickened and her heartbeat jumped into a rhythm so fast and hard, it stole her breath.

But who cared about breathing when his hands were on her?

His palms cupped her breasts, his fingers circling and tugging on her hardened nipples. Every touch sent her rocketing higher and higher on her quest toward a release she knew would leave her staggered.

He dipped his head and claimed first one nipple and then the next, working each hardened, sensitive bud with his tongue and teeth. Nibbling, tasting, suckling until she held his head to her and moved into his mouth, wanting so much more, wanting him. She *needed.* Needed with every cell in her body. Needed with all that she was, all that she might be.

Give yourself to me, querida.

His words tumbled through her fragmented mind and Erin clung to them as she would a life ring tossed into a churning ocean. His need for her was as a finely wrought silver chain, binding her to him and she wanted those bonds tightly formed. She wanted to be a part of him, feel him become a part of her.

Take me, Ricardo. Take me and let me take you.

Opening her eyes, she looked at him as he drew on her breast, sending out deeply felt, tugging sensations that were so overwhelming it felt as though he were drawing her very soul into his body. He ran the edges of his teeth over her skin and Erin hissed in a breath, hoping it was enough, knowing she couldn't draw another. He groaned, tonguing her nipples, one after the other. Her heart opened and splintered in front of him. She was his. She could not imagine belonging to anyone else.

His head lifted at her thought. *No,* he whispered into her mind. *There are no others. Only me. There is only us.*

He slid one hand down the length of her body, to the juncture of her thighs. She held her breath. He touched her. Erin lifted her hips off the bed, rising to meet his questing fingers, parting her thighs in silent welcome. In silent plea.

Only us. She looked into his eyes as he dipped his fingers into her tight, hot channel. She gasped as he withdrew and dipped within again. Held by the power of his silvery gaze, she could do no more than watch him as he took her.

His gaze captured hers and fed the fires raging within her. His hunger was hers. His need, hers. They were one, bound in body and mind.

Again and again, his fingers claimed her, mimicking the act of love, showing her what was to come. His thumb stroked that one small bud of hardened desire at her core and Erin shrieked, jerking in his grasp as the melding sensations poured over her in a river of unending heat. His fingers pressed on her from the inside, his thumb stroked her center and when she thought she might simply die from sensory overload, he took her that one last step and held her as she flew over the edge of need into sated oblivion.

Ricardo...

Again, he whispered into her mind. *Always again.*

Her body was still trembling. Sparks flared inside her, shivering through her bloodstream, making her body shiver and her soul tremble.

She couldn't. Not again. Not so soon. It was too much. Too strong. But he gave her no choice. She watched him dip his head to her breast again and then held her breath as he slid down the length of her body, his mouth and tongue blazing a trail of fire that seemed to incinerate her flesh.

"Oh, God, Ricardo," she said, her voice broken, her ability to steal into his mind gone for the moment, stolen by her body's imminent collapse. "I can't. It's too much."

It is not enough, querida. *It will never be enough.*

He slid off the edge of the bed and knelt on the floor. Tugging her closer, she slid to him on the elegant sweep of silk, helpless to stop him. Knowing she didn't *want* to stop him. If she died from sheer pleasure, it would be a small price to pay.

Parting her thighs, he draped her legs across his shoulders. His big, strong hands kneaded the soft flesh of her bottom as he lifted her to his mouth. *I want all of you, Erin. I must have you,* he whispered into her mind and bent his head to claim her heat in the most intimate way possible. Erin sucked in air like a drowning victim and fisted her hands in the pale blue silk beneath her.

Fly for me.

And she did.

His mouth covered her heat. His tongue slid over incredibly sensitive flesh and brand new, demanding desire was born inside her. She moved into him, against him, wriggling on the cool blue silk. His hands held her bottom, his fingers hot on her skin. She writhed against him, helpless to ease the ache building inside her.

It was more than she'd ever known. More than she would have believed possible. He touched her in ways she had never expected. Moved her to feel things she had never imagined.

Sensation after sensation roared through her, stoking her body into a roiling bonfire that filled her with heat. Her hips lifted and fell of their own accord. His hands held her, pinned to his mouth and oh-so-talented tongue.

Erin gasped, struggling for air, fighting for each breath so that she could keep going, keep feeling what he was doing to her. Reaching down, she fisted her hands in his hair and held his mouth to her as if half afraid he would stop. Again and again, his tongue moved over her most delicate flesh. Tasted her, sighed into her, gave and took more than Erin had known existed.

Ricardo… It was a sigh in her mind. His name sliding through her with a power all its own. She stared blindly up at the ceiling as moonlight cast shadows swayed and dipped, in an erotic dance that only fed the wild craving within.

Santos caught the images in her mind and sent her back more pictures, each of them vivid, stark in their need. *His body plunging into hers. Her atop him, riding him with wild abandon as wave after wave of sensual delight washed over her. Again and again, he showed her what he wanted to do to her, with her.*

Erin sucked in air desperately, as her mind, her body, her soul, focused solely on what Santos was doing to her. What he was *going* to do to her. What he was making her feel.

Then, shifting her gaze to him, she gasped as she watched him take her. His mouth on her, his hands gripping her behind, each fingertip burning a brand on her flesh as surely as he had branded himself on her mind.

He was a shadow within her. She felt his presence in her mind as completely as she felt his mouth on her body. Each stroke of his tongue, each sigh of his breath pushed her higher, higher than she had been before. Higher than she had believed she could go. And she wanted more. Wanted to be lost in this moment, captured for all time.

The intensity of the feelings he created were incredible. Her body coiled, ready to explode. Erin immersed herself in it, allowing her mind to fade away, her will, her spirit, all of it was sublimated to what he was doing to her.

As her body tightened, flashed into an earth-shattering explosion, she held his mouth to her and cried his name on a broken sigh of ecstasy.

And before the last ripple of wonder had coursed through her, Santos had moved, snatching her off the bed, wrapping her in his strong arms, holding her pressed against him. He kissed her, tangling his tongue with hers, as he used one hand to guide her legs around his waist. Then he tore his mouth from hers, looked down into her eyes and said, "Take me. Take me inside you."

Beyond desire now, well into madness, Erin could only agree. Her body was no longer hers, but his. He had claimed it, made it his own and she wanted nothing more than to feel his body sliding into hers.

Instantly, the bond between them strengthened even further. Erin knew him. Saw his life, his centuries of service to the mortal world. She felt him deep within her and knew that he was even deeper than even she could imagine.

She hooked her legs around his hips, threw her arms around his neck and rose up, up, her gaze never leaving his. Erin stared into that magical swirl of silver as she slowly lowered herself onto his thick, hard shaft. Inch by incredible inch, she took him inside her.

She felt her body stretch and give, making way for the fullness of him. When she had taken all of him, he hissed in a short, sharp breath and took a step back, to brace himself against the wall.

Then using his unbelievable strength, he guided her movements, lifting her, then lowering her back down again. He set the pace, locked in a rhythm that seemed to mimic that of their racing hearts. Again and again, she took him within, feeling him fill her. Feeling him fill all the dark and empty places within. All the lonely corners of her life that had, until now, felt like shadows on her soul.

He was everywhere. In her mind, in her body and Erin couldn't get enough of him. Deeper and deeper he delved, pushing himself higher, farther into her hot, tight body.

It is you, querida, he reached for her mind. *You who are banishing the shadows.*

With that thought, those words singing through her mind, Erin kissed him and held him tightly as her body shuddered into another cataclysmic release. But this time, she didn't go alone. This time, she felt Santos's jubilant, silent shout as he reached that peak with her.

"Protect her, fools!" The deep voice rolled out over the watching crowd with the force of a clap of thunder. "If their plan succeeds, if the mortals kill her before her birthday, all is lost. I have not waited thirty years for her powers to be foiled now, when victory is so close at hand."

A few bowed their heads, glances sliding from side to side uneasily, no one willing to meet the great one's gaze. Swirls of smoke and heat stretched across the room like grasping fingers and those in the crowd edged farther back, careful not to draw attention to themselves.

He spoke again, his voice still loud enough, strong enough, to rattle the very gates of hell. "Send someone to protect her until it is time. And if you fail…" He paused, his glittering red gaze sweeping the faces of those who served him. "Soon, we will have all we have waited centuries for. Soon, the power will be mine and I will grind my enemies into dust." He whirled away, stalking into the fiery lit darkness, his fury all that remained to hang like a physical threat in the cavernous room.

* * *

"That was…amazing," Erin said softly, staring up at the tossing, twisting shadows on the ceiling. Turning her head on the pillow, she looked at Santos.

His hand slid up her body to cup one of her breasts and her skin, still tingling with sensation, felt as though it was on fire. "We have Mated."

"Yeah," she said, sighing again. "I noticed."

"No." He went up on one elbow and looked down into her eyes. "There was more than the simple joining of our bodies. Did you not feel it?"

Everything in her went still and quiet. "I felt… something different."

He smoothed her hair back from her face and his dark eyes connected with hers and held. "There is an ancient legend among the Guardians."

She looked at him and her mind slipped into his with ease, seeing his thoughts before he could even speak them. "Destined Mates?"

"Yes." He didn't look happy about it, either.

Erin's stomach did a fast pitch and roll, then settled again. "Are you telling me that we're—"

"Bonded, yes." Santos pushed off the bed and walked naked to the open French doors. Standing with hands on his hips, he stared out into the night for a long moment before turning his head to look at her over his shoulder. "Each time we come together, we will become stronger. If you do not feel it yet, you will. Soon. Your psychic abilities will grow, even as my strengths as a Guardian will increase."

Erin scooted up on the pillows until she was sitting on the bed, watching him. Picking up the edge of the duvet, she drew it across her body so she wouldn't feel quite so vulnerable. "You're stronger because of me."

"Yes."

"And did you know about this Mates thing *before* we—" She waved a hand at the bed.

"I suspected."

"But you didn't think it was worth mentioning?"

He shoved one hand through his thick black hair and muttered something in Spanish. "I did not believe. I thought..."

"What?"

"I believed my own feelings for you were blurring my thoughts."

A tiny curl of pleasure unwound in her chest, loosening the steel bands around her rib cage. At least he felt something for her. That was something.

"What does the Mate thing mean for us?"

He shook his head, gritted his teeth and said, "According to legend, we were meant to be together."

Erin took a breath and let it slide from her lungs in a slow rush. She cared for him. More than she had expected to. More than she had been prepared for. But she didn't need to read his mind to know that he wasn't interested in being connected to her. A moment later, he spoke and confirmed what she already knew.

"But I am not a man to give his life over to the workings of fate, *querida*," he said, his voice colder now, detached, as if he were already separating himself from her. "We are individuals. Not pawns of a legend more ancient even than I."

"Meaning?" Erin whispered the word.

"Meaning," he said, stalking back to the side of the bed, "when your life is safe again, we will part company. Each of us back to our own worlds."

His eyes were so dark, so empty, Erin shivered. Only moments ago, she'd been surrounded by his warmth. Now, it was as if none of that had happened. Santos was going to keep his heart from her.

Maybe though, she thought, realizing that her own time was running out, that was for the best. If he couldn't save her—if she died on her birthday—he wouldn't mourn her as he would if he allowed himself to care.

"The safeguards will hold," Amy said, slamming a tea kettle onto the stove with enough force to slosh water from the spout.

"No one said they wouldn't," her husband offered, keeping far away from the woman he loved.

"If I'd known what we were up against—" Amy shot a glare at Erin "—I'd have had them stronger in the beginning."

"I didn't know, either, remember?" Erin said.

Afternoon sunlight speared through the high kitchen window and lay in golden slashes across the gleaming oak table.

"I didn't say you did," Amy snapped, slapping tea cups and saucers onto the table with the gentle care of Sherman marching through Richmond. "All I'm saying is, I can't very well erect safeguards if I don't know what I'm fighting."

"Santos said—"

Amy shot her husband a look that had his eyebrows lifting and his gaze dropping to the newspaper spread out on the table in front of him.

"Santos is the one who should have known what he was inviting into the house. As a Guardian, it's his responsibility to—"

Erin sighed and tuned out the rest of her rant. It seemed she was back on Amy's wrong side. Now that she knew the other woman was a witch, Erin was eager to make friends again. The entire household had been on red alert for days and tensions were higher than usual. It had been three days since Maggie had come to the house with murder on her mind. Three days since Erin and Santos had first come together.

And those three days were, in some ways, better than any she had ever known. Yes, the sex was spectacular. Every time she was with Ricardo, she felt their connection deepen, strengthen. She knew darn well she should be keeping her distance from him—but truth be told, she didn't want to. In the weirdness that was her life, he had become something of an anchor. The one steady and true point in her life and she needed him now more than ever.

As he'd promised, her psychic abilities were

growing. When she experienced visions now, they were richer, deeper, more vivid.

Yet…there could be no soft sighs and dreams of a nebulous future. And the more she came to care for Santos the more she realized how much she was going to miss him when their time together was over. But she wouldn't stay with a man who didn't want her.

Besides, until the danger had passed, how could she be sure that what she was feeling for Santos wasn't just an adrenaline-born lust that felt like more because she needed it to be more?

Amy set a delicate, bone china teapot in the middle of the table and scooped loose tea into the pot. Then she paused, took a long breath and closed her eyes as she released that pent up breath in a long, slow rush. "I'm sorry. Both of you." She shrugged, shook her head and said, "It's only that I feel stupid. And foolish. That old woman spiked our tea and I never saw it coming."

"It wasn't your fault, Amy," Erin said. "I trusted Maggie my whole life. I thought she loved me."

Wincing, Amy glanced at her. "I'm sorry for that, as well. It couldn't have been easy for you and I'm sure I'm making it no easier."

"Doesn't matter," Erin said and pulled out a

chair to sit down. The kitchen was a warm, friendly room and she felt more at home here than she did in any other part of the Cliffside mansion. Except, of course, for the master bedroom.

She shivered, wrapped her arms around her and asked, "Did Santos say when he'd be back?"

"No," Thomas answered and laid the paper down. "He was going to take the old woman's dagger to the university library. See if anyone recognizes the scrollwork on it."

"He should have let me touch it," Erin said, irritated all over again. Yes, Ricardo Santos was an amazing lover. He made her feel things she hadn't known she was capable of. But he was also arrogant, hardheaded and bossy. A true man of his time, Santos wanted to keep women safe on a tidy little pedestal. He may have lived for hundreds of years, seen the times and people change around him, but he was still firmly lodged in the fifteenth century.

God. That she could even think that and believe it. She was falling in love with a man who had seen the rise and fall of empires. Lived through more changes in the world than she could even comprehend.

And, she reminded herself, though it was her

life at stake, Santos seemed determined to keep her out of whatever it was he was planning. Well, he was going to have a fight on his hand. Erin wouldn't lay down and die. Just as she wouldn't allow someone else to fight her battles for her.

"I told him I could probably have seen its entire history with one touch."

"That's exactly what he didn't want," Amy said before Thomas could. She lifted the steaming kettle off the stove, and poured the boiling water into the waiting teapot. Once it was full, she set the kettle back onto the stove and covered the teapot with a hand-knitted cozy. Taking a seat opposite Erin, she said, "He told you why. He didn't want you risking yourself. If that dagger is as old as we think it is, it's possible the thing has been used to kill hundreds, maybe thousands of people. He didn't want your mind tested with that much tragedy."

"Neither do I," Erin assured her. "But at the same time, if I can figure out what the significance of the dagger is, maybe we can end all of this before the *next* attack comes."

Amy sniffed and lifted her chin. "There'll not be another attack on *this* house. No one will be getting through the wards I set around the perimeter. Absolutely *no one* is getting into this house."

The kitchen door swung open and a tall, broad man with black hair, blue eyes and a hard look to his jaw stepped inside. "Where's Santos?"

Chapter 9

Erin bolted out of her chair and stared at the huge man standing in the open doorway. He was silhouetted against the afternoon sunlight that streamed around the edges of his body, gilding him in a golden light that only made him look more powerful than he no doubt was already.

"Bloody hell!" Thomas leaped to his feet, his chair clattering to the floor in a clash of sound.

Amy jumped up, too. Her wide blue eyes fixed on the big man, she whispered to herself, waved her arms in a wide half circle and energy crackled in the air. While her long-fingered hands danced elegantly in front of her, sketching out intricate patterns, her short, spiky hair ruffled in an unseen wind and her eyes narrowed on the intruder.

The big man frowned at all of them, lifted one hand and touched the empty air in front of him. Instantly, he hissed in a breath as if he'd touched a live electrical field. "Damn it, woman, stop your spelling. I'm not the enemy."

Amy didn't stop. Didn't even slow down. Determined not to be caught off guard again, she built an invisible wall of safeguards between the three of them and the unknown man.

"Then who the hell are you?" Thomas demanded.

"Nicolo Marsini," he muttered, flicking a finger at the energy wall in front of him. Sparks flew. "A Guardian."

Erin's breath slid from her lungs on a slow rush of relief. She dropped one hand to the back of the closest chair and leaned into it. Her knees felt like water and her blood still pumped with adrenaline. Her heartbeat was thundering in her chest and her mouth was dry.

Fear faded slowly, easing out of her body as if reluctant to leave completely. And why should it? Just because this man wasn't a threat, didn't negate the fact that *someone* was still after her. *Someone* still wanted her dead.

"Leave off, witch," the man demanded, still watching Amy as if he half expected her to lift off the floor and fly about the room. "I'm no threat to any of you."

Slowly, Amy allowed the rush of energy to drain away. The energy crackling around her softened until there was only a whiff of power lingering in the motionless air.

"Santos didn't tell us you were coming," Thomas said, warily keeping an eye on the intruder as he moved to stand between his wife and the other man.

"Because he did not know," Nicolo said, his black gaze drifting until it settled on Erin. He studied her for a long minute, then nodded his head slowly, gave her a smile that disappeared as he turned back to the couple in front of him.

Erin felt the power of him seething into the room. Were all Guardians this...*intense?* The strength of the man seemed to take up all the space in the room. His presence alone was powerful, intimidating. But though she was aware of him as an incredibly gorgeous, almost too good-looking man, there was none of the "magic" she felt whenever Santos was near.

"Where is the old Spaniard? Why is he not here to defend this house himself?" Nicolo stepped into the room, slammed the door behind him and shrugged out of the long black coat he wore. A sword was strapped to his side and Erin wondered if all Guardians were so equipped. For some reason, she'd suspected that Santos carried a sword because it had been the weapon he was most familiar with. But then, maybe Nicolo, too, was centuries old.

God, her life had become a sci-fi movie.

"He is right in front of you, you Sicilian fool." Santos's voice thundered into the room and everyone there turned toward the sound. The air shimmered, spun and suddenly, Santos was there, with them. His black eyes went first to Erin, as if assuring himself she was all right. Then he looked back at the man frowning at him.

"Do you often use your shield when in your own home?" Nicolo asked, laughing as he stretched out one hand to him.

"Only when I must see for myself that it is a friend approaching the house, not an enemy." Santos took the other man's hand in a firm grip and smiled at him. "It has been too long, Nicolo."

Erin pulled out the chair she'd been leaning on and plopped down into it. Thomas sat down, too, while Amy suddenly burst into activity, bustling around the kitchen, gathering two more cups and saucers and setting the teakettle back to boil.

"I'm on my way home," Nicolo said, leaning one shoulder against the bank of cabinets beside him. He hooked his thumbs into the black belt at his waist and said, "My demon ran to Mexico. Thought to lose me in the crowds. But I found it in Rosarita. Its trip to Hell was not a pleasant one."

"Problems?" Santos asked, one eyebrow lifting.

"Nothing more than usual," he said. "I thought to stay here to relax for a few days before leaving for Sicily. But it seems," he added, with a sweeping stare at the still shaken people in the room, "that there is little chance of relaxation here."

"There is something going on," Santos admitted, yanking the leather tie from the nape of his neck to allow his shoulder-length black hair to hang loose. He shifted a look at Erin and felt his pulse pound in response.

He felt her slowly ebbing fear mingled with a fascination at the friendship between Santos and Nicolo. A fast eruption of jealousy clouded his mind, then dissipated almost as quickly as it had appeared. She wasn't attracted to the other

Guardian. He knew that by the strength of her thoughts. But there was curiosity and interest.

And fear. The constant shadow of fear lurked deeply in her brain and frustration flooded Santos. He hated that he hadn't been able to help her yet. He was a man used to accomplishing any task he set for himself. He had survived centuries on his wit and his strengths. The fact that he hadn't yet disposed of the threat to her gnawed at him.

But it was more than that and he knew it. Carefully blocking his thoughts from hers, Santos silently admitted that their connection—his and Erin's—was stronger than ever. He felt it with every breath. At night, his mind reached for hers and their dreams entwined. On waking, his mind again reached for hers as if he were unable to take up his day without first reassuring himself that Erin was well and with him.

He didn't want this.

Didn't want to be so entangled with a woman that he no longer felt whole without her. Not again. Didn't want to be tied to one woman throughout eternity. And yet…he could no longer imagine his too-long life without her in it.

The legend of Destined Mates rose up in his

mind again and Santos gritted his teeth. Only a short time ago, he had laughed at his friend Kieran MacIntyre's misery on finding *his* Destined Mate. He'd enjoyed the other Guardian's frustration and helplessness in the face of a woman who had brought the ancient Scot to his knees.

Now, it seemed, Fate was laughing at Santos.

But he would have the last laugh, he assured himself. He would save Erin. Defeat the enemies threatening her. And then he would set her free. Let her move back to her own life and with time, they would forget about each other. It was best that way, he assured himself. He wouldn't be able to concentrate on his sacred duty if he were to have a woman as part of his life. And Erin deserved more than to live with a man who would never age, even as she grew old and died. Though a small voice in the back of his mind reminded him that he could, at any time, choose to become a mortal, he knew that he couldn't do it.

He was a warrior.

It was what he knew.

All he knew.

Scraping one hand across his jaw, Santos turned his attention to his old friend and tried to ignore the racing beat of Erin's heart pounding in his head.

"Come into the study," Santos said. "We will talk."

Nicolo's features stiffened as if he could sense the gravity of the problems facing Santos. Nodding, he said, "I am at your disposal until I return to Sicily." The teakettle screamed into the silence. Giving the steam rising from the spout a sneer, he added, "I will do what I can, but I will not drink tea."

Amy sniffed in disapproval.

But Santos laughed and clapped one hand on the Sicilian's shoulder. "Red wine or white?"

Nicolo looked appalled. "*Red,* of course."

"Come then. We will drink and plot together."

A half hour later, Erin hovered outside the closed study door. She'd followed the men to the study minutes after they'd left the kitchen, but now, she was waiting, trying to hear what was going on inside the closed room. She couldn't reach Santos's thoughts and that worried her. She was so used to being able to communicate with him silently, finding that path blocked to her made her feel more alone than she ever had in her life.

What was he thinking that he didn't want her to know? Had he discovered something about the

knife? About those who were after her? And if he
had, why wasn't he sharing it with her? Why
would he talk to this Guardian—who had nothing
at all to do with the situation—and *not* include
her? After all, wasn't it *her* life at stake here?

She pressed her ear to the door, but all she heard
was a soft mutter of sound. Nothing to cling to.
Nothing to give her the peace she needed so desperately. Frustration brewed in the pit of her
stomach, fed by a rising tide of annoyance. She
wasn't a child to be put aside and patted on the
head. She wasn't a fool to be soothed by the
promise of safety. She wasn't a woman who
would allow someone else—no matter how well-
meaning—to make her decisions for her.

With that thought firmly in mind, Erin grabbed
the cold brass knob, gave it a turn and pushed the
door open. She stood on the threshold, looking at
the two men and for just one moment, she was absolutely awed by them. Standing in front of the
hearth, they appeared as if they had been plucked
from the pages of history. Warriors of old, they
looked as though they were ready to do battle with
dragons or barbarians. And she had no doubt that
they would win whatever battle they engaged in.

Each of them wore black. Each of them were

muscled and strong and taller than most men. Each of them seemed to pulse with power. And each of them turned to look at her with impatience etched into their features.

But Erin wouldn't be cowed. Lifting her chin, she said, "If you're discussing me, then I should be a part of the conversation."

Nicolo scowled. "Women do not belong in talks of battle."

"Welcome to the twenty-first century," she snapped. Shifting her gaze to Santos, she spoke directly into his mind, so that only he would hear. *Don't hide the danger from me. How can I save myself if I don't know what's happening?*

Querida, he answered, his voice whispering into her mind, *you need not save yourself. I am here.*

Oh, don't get me wrong, I welcome the help. But, she shook her head. "This is important to me. I have to be a part of it."

He nodded and stretched out one hand toward her. "Come then."

"This is a mistake." Nicolo drained the last of the red wine in his glass and reached for the bottle on a nearby table. Splashing more of the ruby liquid into the fine crystal glass, he shook his head grimly. "The woman will only complicate this further."

Erin walked directly to Santos. Standing close to him, she looked at the other man. "It's my life," she reminded him.

"And it falls to Santos to protect that life."

"With my help."

"*¡Silencio!*" Santos's voice thundered out around them and got the response he had been looking for. The only sound in the room was the hiss and snap of the flames on the logs. Taking Erin's hand, he guided her to one of the chairs and eased her down into it. *Nicolo is not used to anyone interfering with his plans.*

And you are? she asked.

No, he admitted, *but at least I am more accustomed to dealing with you.*

"This is a mistake," Nicolo said again with a long drink of his wine.

"Then it is mine to worry about," Santos told him, effectively ending the argument.

Erin chose to ignore the other Guardian. She felt his irritation simmering around him, but that was his problem. For now, she wanted to know what Santos had found out about the knife.

"Did you learn anything at the university?" she asked.

Santos pulled the antique dagger from a loop

at his belt and held it balanced on the palm of one hand. "Less than I would have liked," he admitted with a frown. He glanced at her and couldn't hide the shadows in his eyes from her. "There is an antiquities department there. The professor examined it, but he had never seen anything like it."

"So then, nothing new." Erin slumped into the chair, letting the overstuffed piece surround her with comfort.

Nicolo bent down, grabbed a poker and jabbed at the fire, sending a shower of sparks up the chimney in a swirl of flashing lights.

"Only one thing," Santos admitted, his gaze now on Erin, dismissing Nicolo as if he weren't there at all. "The professor said the scrollwork, the design, looked Celtic in origin."

"Celtic?" Erin rubbed her temples and tried to think, but her mind was a jumble of thoughts, images, fears. "Well," she said softly as a pattern began to lay itself out in her brain, "Maggie was Irish. My adoptive family was. Even my birth mother." She lifted her gaze to Santos's. "But what does it all mean?"

"It means only that we must now turn to Ireland," Nicolo said, standing up to look at Erin again. "If mortals and demons alike are after you, then this is unlike anything we have come across before."

"Oh," she whispered, finally understanding the old saying "her heart sank." It felt as though her own heart had dropped right down to the soles of her feet. "That's just great news."

"There is a way to find answers…" Nicolo muttered.

Santos shot him a glare that would have killed anyone who wasn't immortal.

"What?" Erin demanded, looking from one man to the other, waiting for *someone* to explain what they were talking about.

"It is nothing," Santos said, his voice tight and hard, an audible fist aimed at his friend.

"Fine, Spaniard," Nicolo said, setting his wine-glass down with a heavy clunk of crystal on wood. His dark eyes narrowed and his jaw clenched. "This is your challenge. We will abide by your rules."

Santos ignored the other man, closed his fist around the hilt of the knife, bent down and leaned in to lock his gaze with Erin's. "Do not mind the Sicilian. I know you are frightened, but you should know…*believe*…that I will keep you safe. I will allow no one to harm you."

"Time is running out," she whispered. "There are only two weeks until my birthday. And if these people are determined to reach me before then, the attacks are going to come more often. You heard Maggie. Before she died she said they won't give up. They won't stop until I'm dead."

Santos set the knife down on the table, lifted her easily and sat down himself, holding her on his lap. She curled into the warm, solid strength of him and it was like cuddling up to a brick wall. His body was hard, solid, and she knew every inch of it as thoroughly as she knew her own.

Laying her head on his chest, Erin closed her eyes and sighed, secure for the moment with his arms around her. The world outside this room was frightening. The enemies stacked against her were many.

But in Santos's arms, she felt hope. She felt safe.

Barely aware of the other man, Erin heard Nicolo's steps as he quietly left the room and closed the door behind him. Alone with Santos, she whispered, "Your friend doesn't like me much."

"He doesn't like the situation," Santos corrected. "Nor do I."

She lifted her head so that she could look into his eyes again. "What're we going to do?"

"We are going to solve this. We are going to give you back your life."

Erin frowned suddenly as his thoughts shimmered in her mind. *And then you will leave me. We will part, return to our own worlds, as is only right.*

"What is it?" he asked, running the tips of his fingers down the line of her jaw.

Instead of answering, she listened to his thoughts, open to her now. Whatever block he had been using before was now forgotten—and a moment later, she wished it were still in place.

His thoughts were clear, firm. *I do not want to want you. I do not have room for this in my life. Mine is a world of battles where a woman cannot belong. You must leave. You must find your own way and I mine.*

Until then though, I will protect you and give you all that I can.

A part of her heart died quietly, aching with a wrenching agony that rocked her with its power. She hadn't even been aware just how her feelings for Santos had taken root and grown. She hadn't realized how deeply she'd come to care for him. How much she needed the physical and mental connection she had found with him.

Hearing him regret the very thing she cherished, she felt pain like nothing she'd ever known before.

Erin? His voice came as a sigh in her mind. *I see the worry in your eyes. Do not. Do not surrender to the fear that surrounds you. I will be here with you. Always.*

Or, she thought with a sad pang of regret, until you free me and let me go. Carefully, she hid her thoughts from him, as he had shown her only a few days ago. She couldn't bear to see pity in his eyes as he realized she knew that he didn't want her.

Instead, her hands cupped his face, her eyes studied his. Her fingers smoothed over his skin, loving the feel of him, *needing* him that moment more than she could stand. If she were only to have him in her life for a short time, then she would revel in him while she could.

Moving in close, she laid her mouth over his, smoothed her tongue across his lips. He hissed in a breath and his arms tightened around her reflexively. She nibbled at his mouth and her hands moved down to the buttons on his shirt. Undoing them quickly, she slid her palms beneath the silky black fabric to caress the brown muscled flesh she knew so well.

Maybe she was being an idiot. Being with him would only make their inevitable parting that much harder. But how could she not touch him and be touched while she still had the chance?

He kissed her hard, thrusting his tongue into her depths, tasting, claiming. His breath became hers, her soul sighed into his. She felt their connection deeply, right down to her bones. Whether he wanted to keep her in his life or not, Erin knew that he would never forget her. Would never be able to push the memories of them together from his mind.

And in that moment, she knew she wanted to make it as difficult as possible for him to let her go.

She pulled her mouth from his. Shifting on his lap, she kneeled astride him and pulled the hem of her skirt up, up, slowly, temptingly. Baring her thighs to him, she watched as his dark eyes swirled silver with need and she knew that at this moment, he wanted her as much as she did him.

"Erin…"

"I need you, Ricardo." Her words came on a whispered sigh.

"As I do you."

His hands moved up the length of her thighs,

fingertips sliding across her skin, sending shivers of delight coursing through her veins like hot, thick lava rolling down the side of a volcano. And that's what she felt like. A volcano. With her own desires bubbling and quickening inside her, threatening to erupt and spill over him.

"Querida," he whispered, *"eres hermosa."*

Erin smiled faintly. *Translate, Ricardo.*

Beautiful, he sighed into her thoughts, *you are beautiful.*

She looked down into his eyes and actually felt beautiful for the first time in her life. She read his emotions plainly on his face and shared them all. Need. Desire. Want. And for her, there was more. There was love.

Erin felt her world rock and tilt on its axis. This she hadn't admitted to herself before. In fact, she had avoided looking too closely at the affection she held for him, knowing that her life was in turmoil. Expecting that in the midst of danger, emotions ran high and lust could be mistaken for more.

But she was sure now.

She loved Ricardo Santos.

Loved a man who wanted her gone.

Her heart ached.

Her body burned.

He tore her silk panties free of her body and cupped her heat, one finger diving within her slick, tight channel. She swayed, unsteady on her knees, unsteady in her mind, her heart.

He was all. He was everything that had been missing from her life and soon, he would be gone from her. Because she would never stay with a man who didn't want her.

But for now, they were together and she would take all that he was willing to give.

As his fingers plied her deepest places, she reached down, worked the zipper of his slacks down and freed him to her grasp. Hard and long and thick, he was ready for her and Erin's body hungered for his invasion.

Lifting the hem of her blouse up and over her head, Erin looked down at Santos and read the wild hunger in his eyes. He unclasped her bra, spilling her heavy breasts into his palms. His thumbs moved across the rigid, pink tips and Erin sighed his name.

Now, querida. *Take me within you now.*

Keeping her gaze locked with his, she lowered herself onto him, taking him into her body slowly, languidly, as if to belie the frenzied need whipping through her. When he was buried fully within her, she twisted her hips atop him, increasing the need, jolting them both with the friction of two heated bodies sliding together. She made them both ache. She pushed the magic between them into an incredibly raw, frantic dance of desire.

They moved as one, their mouths linked, their bodies joined, their minds connected in a hazy blur of want. His hands at her hips, he guided her every move and thrust himself into her depths. Erin braced her hands on his shoulders, gazed into his eyes and lost herself in the swirl of silvery passion. She moved on him in a rhythm that matched the pounding of their hearts, joining them yet again in the most elemental way possible.

As the tightened coil inside her splintered into a million jagged pieces, Erin tipped her head back, sighed his name on a cry of wonder and heard him whisper throatily into her mind.

Te amo, querida. Te amo.

Chapter 10

"What?"

Santos went absolutely still. Staring up into the emerald-green eyes he knew as well as he knew his own, he saw them flash and knew he'd spoken aloud. Yet even as he silently berated himself for speaking, he realized that even if he hadn't, she would have heard him think the words that had slipped up on him.

Pulling her close, he wrapped his arms around her and held her pressed to his chest. Their bodies still joined, their minds reaching for each other, he couldn't hide his feelings from her and would not have if he could have chosen.

She deserved to know what he felt for her, even if those feelings would not change his decision about their future.

Resting his cheek on top of her head, he sighed and whispered, "Yes, I love you."

"That works out well then," she said, her words muffled slightly against his chest, "because I love you, too."

For one brief moment, he held those softly spoken words close to his heart. In centuries of living, he had never heard them before. Not even in his first lifetime. Not even from the woman to whom he'd given so much. To find this gift now, when he couldn't—*wouldn't*—accept it, was almost physically painful.

"Ricardo…?" She moved in his grasp, lifting her head to look up at him. "I know this is fast. And trust me, I didn't really believe it at first, either. I mean," she said, pushing her hair back from her face with an impatient hand, "I've only known you a week. But somehow, it feels like I've *always* known you."

"I feel this, as well, Erin." Her eyes sparkled with light, with love, and it took every ounce of strength she had gifted him with to steel himself against it. "I am drawn to you as to no other. I never believed in the Guardian's legend of Mates. Until you."

"But…" she said it for him when he didn't.

"Erin."

She studied him for a long moment. "You don't want me."

"I do," he assured her, capturing her face between his palms, his thumbs stroking her skin. "I do want you, *querida.*" He was unable to lie when staring into her eyes. And even if he could, he wouldn't lie to her. Not to Erin. Not about this. "See my thoughts, know what I think and feel."

"I have," she said, carefully disentangling their bodies. He felt suddenly cold and alone.

She stepped away from him, straightened the fall of her skirt and walked to the fireplace. Staring into the flames, she said quietly, "I heard your thoughts. I know you feel there's no place for me in your life."

He stood, adjusted his own clothing and kept his gaze fixed on her. His every instinct was to go to her, pull her into his arms and hold her so closely she could never escape him. Yet he knew that wasn't the answer. He watched her, the curvy lines of her body, the sweep of her dark red hair, flashing bright in the firelight. She was…unexpected in his life.

Perhaps, he thought, that was why he was handling this all so badly. He walked over to join her. Taking her arm, he turned her to face him and was almost lost in the sheen of tears in her eyes. She had come to him for help. Had trusted him with her very life. And now he had brought her to the brink of tears.

"*Querida,* if I were a different man, I would keep you with me always." His voice was soft, yet firm. He wanted her to hear him. Believe him. Know what it cost him to let her go. "But I am a warrior. It is all I know. All I have ever known. I would not have you be a part of that."

"Aren't I already a part of it?" she demanded. "Someone is trying to kill me. I'm caught in this little battle whether you want to admit it or not."

"Yes. You are. But you will not be caught in any of the ones that follow." His hand tightened on her arm. "My life is a series of battles. One following the other. There is always another demon. Always another war to be fought. I wish you to have a life separate from that. To have a normal life."

She actually laughed as she tugged her arm free of his grasp. "I've never had a *normal* life," she said, her voice rising even as her eyes flashed at him dangerously. "You've seen my memories. You know what I've experienced, what I've felt. I've helped the police find killers. I've touched an object belonging to a 'friend' only to find out that they weren't my friends at all. I dip into people's pasts, am haunted by their mistakes, their regrets. There's nothing 'normal' about that, believe me."

"And yet," he argued, mesmerized by the play of firelight in her eyes, "you live. You work. You have a job you love and a home you enjoy. You make friends. You have lived your life unmindful of the demon threat. You can return to that life, *querida*. You should return to it."

"Because you say so?" She shook her head and took a step back, apparently needing the distance from him. "Don't you see, Ricardo? With or without you in my life, there is no normalcy for me. My mother gave me up at birth. My adoptive parents thought I was a freak of nature. And just look at the last few weeks, for God's sake! I've been stalked, thrown in front of a bus, chased by demons and hunted by a woman I thought *loved* me. I found you, and fell in love with a man who's lived…for centuries…" She paused, took a breath and hurried on. "I can hardly believe any of this is happening. But it *is*. And you sending me home because loving me is inconvenient isn't going to change any of it."

Santos's own temper spiked but he tamped it down deliberately. She wasn't seeing. Didn't know that what he did, he did for *her.* "I have lived many lifetimes. You know that. You came to me knowing that."

"Yes, and—"

"You see the world I live in and think to become a part of it even while it terrifies you. And don't deny it, I can read the fear in your mind."

"Well, of course I'm afraid," Erin snapped, staring at him as though his head were made of concrete. "I'd be a complete idiot to not be scared. But I'm not scared of loving you. Of being with you. I can't even believe I'm saying this, because it's all happened so quickly. But I *know* you, Ricardo. I've seen your thoughts, your desires, your strength of character and your pride. I've lived in your mind as you fought your battles with demons and I know exactly who you are. I'm not a fool. I'm not in love with a daydream. I love *you.* The man you are."

"I never thought to be given such a rare gift," he murmured, his voice low now, rippling over her skin like the soft sigh of a jungle cat. "And I will always treasure it."

She sighed and all of her air left her, like a balloon suddenly popped. "But you will still let me go."

"I will," he said and though regret tinged his words, it changed nothing.

Erin sadly accepted that she had lost this battle. She had failed to convince him that they belonged together. That he needed her in his life as much as she did him.

Shaking her head, she said, "You don't have to look so worried. I won't throw myself at you and beg you to let me stay."

Santos winced inwardly at the pain radiating in her thoughts like knives. He had done this. Caused her hurt. When all he had wanted to do was to keep her safe.

"I'll stay until this is settled and then I'll go."

A deep void opened up inside him and though he knew it was stupid to regret what must be, he knew her loss would leave him a broken man. It might be centuries before he could draw a breath without remembering her scent. Before he could reach out his hand in the night and not hope to touch her. Before he would forget the sheen of unshed tears in her eyes at this very moment.

But it was not for himself he would end this. It was for her. Erin's life with him would be one of danger, constant peril, with the threat of the demon world always close at hand. He wanted her to have better. He wanted her safety above all else.

"But what about the Destined Mate thing?" She shifted her gaze from his to stare at the dancing flames in the hearth. "*Can* we be separate?"

"Yes," he said, searching his memories for every nugget of information on the legend of Destined Mates. "Though we are meant to be together, we can each live our lives apart. Some of those meant to be never find each other and live happy lives. It will not be easy at first, but—"

"Spare me. I don't expect things to be easy," she said. "I never have."

"*Querida...*"

She shook her head, brushing away his tenderness as if it was just too much to bear. "Don't, Santos. I'm on the edge here and if you're nice to me..."

How he would miss her. The fire of her spirit. The warmth in her eyes. He smiled sadly, knowing she was withdrawing from him as surely as he must from her. This was his choice, but Santos knew that he faced a lifetime of regret for the making of it.

"As you wish."

She whipped her head around to look at him, astonishment clear on her features. "None of this is as I wish it. I didn't ask to be stalked by some crazy person—and *demons,* for God's sake. I didn't expect to love you. Didn't think it was possible to love someone after knowing them only a week. And I didn't wish for my love to be thrown back in my face."

He met her gaze with a deadly stare, one he had honed and developed over lifetimes of war and battle. He was doing the right thing. For him. For her. Destined Mate or no, Erin Brady was never meant to live in his world. "You must trust me to know what is best in this matter."

Santos stalked through the misty gray of the night. Wispy, straggly fingers of fog whipped apart like fragile fabric as his long legs moved with determined strides. Fury rode him. She did not understand, but how could he expect her to?

His gaze slashed across the darkness of the cove near La Jolla. The beach here was littered with tide pools, caves and more importantly, a portal leading to the demon dimension. Here is where he wanted to be. To feel the pulsing strength of the other side as demons tried to claw their way into his world. To remind himself of his reason for living.

His boots slid across the damp rocks as the incoming tide slapped at him. Beneath his feet, sea creatures lived and died in tide pool kingdoms of their own. Santos felt none of it. Instead, he reached out with his senses, searching for the wash of energy that would lead him to the latest demon to escape its hell.

Anticipation rushed through him as he broke into a run. The long hem of his black coat swung out around him like the wings of a night creature. His gaze fixed on his target, Santos reached for the sword at his side and pulled it free of the scabbard.

With the cold, worn hilt of his sword in his hand, Santos felt the exhilaration of battle rise up inside. This is what he was. What he was always meant to be.

The demon crouched in the fog, nearly bent in half, moved with a sliding, slippery step that made it look more reptile than anything else.

"Hold!" Santos shouted as he leaped from the last boulder separating him from his target. He sailed through the cold, damp air and felt the wind push at him. The demon swiveled its head and snarled, mouth open to display a row of jagged, sharp teeth.

Santos hit the sand hard, rolled and came up directly in front of the demon. His blood pumped, his heart sang as he swung the first blow. The demon leaped back, crashing into the oncoming tide.

Shrieking in fury, it erupted from the cold, frothy sea, with water streaming down its body in sheets. Its fiery red eyes fixed on Santos, the demon charged, hands outstretched, claws curved into deadly talons.

Moonlight glittered in its eyes and Santos swung in a circle, sweeping one leg out, smashing the demon's legs out from under it. Instantly, the creature leaped back up, already recovered. "Guardian…"

Santos lifted his sword, pointed it at heaven and brought it down in a swooping arc. The demon leaped to one side, yet not quickly enough. Dark blood scattered across the sand and the demon's screams echoed in the darkness.

"You have risked much to come here, demon," Santos growled, enjoying himself. Enjoying the thrill of battle.

"And will again should you capture me this night," it said, its voice coming in a halting, sing-song cadence that grated on the ears.

"At your peril," Santos shot back and this time jabbed with the sword, catching the demon high on its side.

Again, the creature howled, this time in fury, not pain, as it sensed victory sliding from its grasp. Santos's blade was merciless. Again and again, he chipped away at the demon's strength, taking small cuts and slashes that drained the demon's will, as well as its blood.

The sand was stained, dark in the moonlight. The water rushed in, wiping away all evidence of the battle even as more blood was spilled. And at last, when the demon admitted defeat, falling beneath one last, mighty blow from Santos's sword, it lay still, staring furiously up at the Immortal who had bested it.

Santos's breath rushed in and out of his lungs. He lifted his face to the wind and let the cold surround him. His hair streamed out behind him, the edge of his coat dipped and swayed and his sword as he jabbed it through the demon's middle, stabbed the wet sand.

"You will return to your world this night, demon."

Laughter spilled from its mouth. Dark, vicious laughter that bubbled from its throat as surely as the blood pooling around it. "But I will heal and come again, Guardian. You have stopped nothing this night. None of your kind can."

"And yet," Santos reminded it, "you are the one lying on the sand, bleeding into the ocean."

"For now." It grabbed at the blade impaling it and when it couldn't pull it free, snarled in fury and lay its head back down onto the sand. "But all we need do is outlast your kind. The last one who fought here ended his life rather than continue the battle. Your time will come. And when it does, this world will be mine."

Rage and regret puddled together in the pit of Santos's stomach. He thought of Stewart, the last protector of this area—then considered the laughing demon before him. Was it right? Would he one day choose Stewart's end? Simply walk away from the duties and responsibilities he had shouldered so long ago?

"You will see," the demon screeched as Santos ripped his blade free and wiped it clean in the incoming tide.

"Perhaps one day, foul one," Santos said tightly. "But not this night."

* * *

Two hours later, Nicolo lunged at Santos and grinned when his opponent deflected his sword blow with a quick parry. Their blades rang in the air like harsh music as the two men came at each other again and again.

The gym at the mansion was well equipped. Everything from free weights to treadmills and ellipticals. There was a mat for sparring and on the walls hung every sort of weapon imaginable. Everything from maces to whips to swords and knives of every conceivable size hung neatly on silver hooks.

"You're slow, old man," Nicolo said, laughing as he made another swipe that Santos easily vaulted over. When he landed in a roll and then sprang to his feet, Santos pressed the tip of his blade to the back of Nicolo's neck.

"Not so old after all, young one."

Nicolo held up one hand, signaling surrender, then turned to face his friend. "Three hundred years isn't so young."

"It is to me," Santos muttered, wiping his blade down with a towel before returning it to its place on the wall.

After his battle with the demon, Santos had

still been too tightly wound to sit easily in the house. Training with Nicolo had seemed like a good way to keep his mind too busy to dwell on thoughts of his conversation with Erin. And yet, it seemed he was well able to both hone his skills and torment himself at the same time.

"So then, Erin must seem like an infant to one as old as you."

Santos turned to glare at the man, but wasn't surprised to see Nicolo brush off the silent reprimand. "Erin is not your concern."

"She shouldn't be yours, either. That's my point. What concerns me is that you have made her your concern." Nicolo dropped onto a weight bench, reaching for a bottle of water. "The woman is trouble. She's brought human killers into this house."

"That is hardly her fault."

Nicolo took a long drink, wiped his forehead with the back of his hand and added, "Even the demon world is after her."

"And it is my duty to protect her."

"Why?" Nicolo stood up, tossed the water bottle and hooked a towel around his neck. Facing Santos, he jammed both hands on his hips and planted his feet in a battle stance. "Why are you protecting her when you don't know the reason they're after her?"

"Why should the reason matter?" Santos stalked the length of the room to the refrigerator, opened it and pulled out a bottle of water. Twisting off the top, he tossed it to one side and downed half the bottle before speaking again. "She needs help. I am a Guardian. It is my duty to protect her."

Nicolo shook his head. "Our duty is to protect the human world from the demon threat."

"Yes."

"What if *she* is the threat?"

Santos snorted. "You are speaking as a fool."

"Am I? Why are humans after her? Why did the demon you last hunted say that the demon world wanted her?"

"She is human. She is in danger. I will stand before her."

"There is something more," Nicolo said, studying his old friend's features. "Something you are not saying."

"Until a new Guardian is assigned to this area," Santos said tightly, "I am in charge. I will make the choices I think best. I do not ask for your help. I do not need your opinions."

"You expect me to return to Sicily and leave you to whatever is coming."

Santos snorted. "You know the law as well as I. One demon, one Guardian. We do not hunt in packs. We are alone, Nicolo. Always alone."

"Not you, though," his friend mused. "Not anymore. Now you have this woman and your concentration is shattered."

Santos sneered at him. That his friend's words reflected much of his own thoughts only served to irritate him further. He would do his duty. He would protect the people of this world from whatever threats presented themselves. And he would protect Erin. Above all, he would see to her safety.

"Did I not just best you in our duel?" Santos reminded him, forcing a smile that felt stiff and unwelcome on his face. "My concentration is fine, Nicolo. You should not test me any further today."

"Your skills are much as they always were," the other man said as he walked to the wall and coolly hung his blade in its proper place. "But your attention is divided, Santos."

He walked back across the room and moved slowly, quietly, danger shimmering around him like an aura. When he stood before Santos again, his expression was cold. Unemotional.

"You are thinking with your dick, Spaniard. And it is something I've never seen you do before."

"Silence." The quiet, deadly fury in his voice was more dangerous a threat than a shout would have been.

"I don't think so," Nicolo continued. "You seem to have forgotten, Santos. Human women are to be laid and then left."

Santos punched him.

Nicolo didn't even stagger under a powerful blow that would have flattened a mortal man. Instead, he smiled as he rubbed his jaw with one hand. "So. There *is* more to her than you are saying."

"Leave it be." Santos clenched his fists at his sides, wanting nothing more than to beat his old friend into the mat. Fury sped through his bloodstream, pumping all through his system in the blink of an eye. He had known and respected the Sicilian for decades. But no one was allowed to dismiss Erin—who and what she was.

As if sensing he'd gone too far, Nicolo said, "If you truly want her protected, you must let her touch the dagger."

"Weren't you the one who said women had no place in talk of battles?"

"I don't say let her fight the demon, only have

her touch the dagger to give us an idea of what you're facing."

"I will find another way."

"This is the best way and you know it to be true." Nicolo backed off, and took a seat on the weight bench. Resting his forearm on his upraised knee, he stared at Santos and said, "You told me she has the gift of sight. She can touch objects and know their history."

Santos's grip tightened on the plastic water bottle. "Yes."

"Then have her touch it. Let her *see* what there is to know of this weapon. When you have the information, you will know what to do."

Santos thought for a few moments before saying, "I don't want her...damaged. The energy surrounding the dagger is intense. Even I can sense the darkness trapped within it."

"Do what you can to ease it, then," Nicolo said quietly. "But if you want to protect her, if you mean to keep her safe, you must discover *why* she is in danger."

Chapter 11

"Why not ask me what I want to do?" Erin's voice came from the doorway and both men turned to look at her.

"Erin, this does not concern you," Santos said grimly.

"Of course it does," she said, moving into the room, ignoring Nicolo and focusing solely on Santos. "I heard your thoughts, Santos. I know that the dagger could be a key to all of this. I want to touch it. I want this over. Finished."

He inclined his head. "It could be dangerous to you."

"It's my decision," Erin said tightly. "Not yours."

"As I have told him," Nicolo muttered.

Erin stiffened at the reminder that they weren't alone. But she didn't look at the other man. Instead, she focused on Santos. On making him see that she needed to do this.

"I want to do what I can. It's important to me. I can't simply hide in this house and hope everything will be taken care of."

Santos reached for her and the moment his hand curled around her forearm, Erin felt his heat zing through her body. Breathtaking, this attraction, this need, that erupted within her any time he was near. She heard his thoughts and knew that he felt just as she did, though he fought the desire that hummed in the air between them.

Deliberately, Erin covered his hand with hers, let him feel her resolve. Let him into her mind so that he could see how important this was to her.

"I must protect you," he whispered, his voice no more than a hush.

"And I have to do what I can to protect myself." *From attack,* she added silently, *and from you. If we can't be together, then I have to leave. Soon.*

His hand on her arm tightened briefly, then he

released her and Erin instantly felt the lack of contact.

"As you wish," he said with another incline of his head.

A half hour later, the household gathered in the study. Amy, surrounded by the crackling energy she evoked with a wave of her hands, set safeguards to protect them all from whatever dangers might possibly be awakened.

Erin hardly noticed. She knew what she had to do, but she so didn't want to. Every time she looked at the knife, she saw Maggie's gaze, alive with fanaticism, focused on her mission to kill Erin. Her heart felt as if it were made of stone. Her stomach was churning. And her mind was a whirl of color and sound, spinning into a tornado of thoughts that had no cohesion beyond fear.

Trembling, she stood beside a table and stared down at the dagger resting on top of it. Mentally, she blocked out the memory of Maggie leaning over her and focused instead on the etched silver designs on the dagger's hilt.

She took a breath and slowly released it, hoping to find the calm she would soon need. A fire roared in the huge hearth and outside, the night pressed against the windows as if trying to find a way inside. Erin's stomach twisted again into dozens of knots, but she drew another deep breath and fought the fear nearly choking her.

She needed to do this. For her own sake.

"Only touch the handle," Santos said from right beside her. "Do not touch the blade."

She nodded, staring down at the dagger. It was beautiful. And old. Even without touching it, Erin could sense the power of the weapon, as if it were a living entity in the room. Touching it might open floodgates she wouldn't be able to close again. Her psychometric powers had grown in the last week or so—Santos had been right about that. Enough that she was more wary than usual about what she might see.

"It's done," Amy announced from the back of the room.

"You should go then," Santos said. "Both of you."

"I'd rather stay," Thomas said.

Erin felt Santos shift to look at the other man. "I am honored that you would risk yourself. But it is better if you take Amy to your quarters."

Thomas hesitated, but finally took Amy's hand and led her from the room.

"You, too, Nicolo."

"I don't need your protection," the Guardian said.

"Nor I yours," Santos snapped. "This is for Erin and I alone to do."

Erin nearly sighed with relief. She hadn't wanted an audience. Hadn't wanted others to see her being swept up into a vision. Santos, yes. Though he had broken her heart, she could trust him to be there for her, no matter what happened.

"Then I will scout the perimeter outside," Nicolo said. "Call if you need assistance."

Once they were all gone and the door closed behind them, Erin looked at Santos. She'd wanted this. But now that the moment was here, her fear was stronger than her need.

"All of a sudden, this doesn't sound like a very good idea," she admitted.

"You do not have to do this," Santos said, reaching out to smooth her hair back from her face. "I have already put in a call to a Guardian I know in Ireland. He is on a hunt, but when he returns, he will call. He may be able to find the information we need without further risk to you."

She sighed at the gentle slide of his fingers against her skin. "I'm grateful you called your friend. But what if he doesn't know anything? I have to do this." She smiled a little. "But thanks for offering me a way out."

His features tightened and a muscle in his jaw ticked. "I will be right here with you."

"Counting on that."

"Then do it and be done," Santos ordered.

"Bossy," she mumbled.

Santos laid one strong hand on her shoulder, joining them as if he could bolster her strength, her courage, with his own. She felt the warmth of his hand seeping into her bones and steeled herself against what was coming. Reaching out, she laid just the tips of her fingers against the intricately carved hilt of the dagger.

Time fell away and Erin with it, as she tumbled into the energy field surrounding the dagger. Erin's heart beat in a wild, frantic rhythm and even through the surging visions rippling through her mind, she instinctively reached for Santos's strength.

He was there, a quiet, reassuring voice in a corner of her mind. She drew on his presence, using it to steady herself amid the whirlwind of sensations pummeling her.

And then a scene erupted around her. Green, a color so rich and vibrant it seemed to have a life all its own. Empty fields and rock walls stretched out all around her. Ancient Ireland. A low, throbbing chant rolled through the air, vibrating against Erin's skin.

She saw a crowd gathered around a straw figure of a man. She felt the people's terror and shared it. From within that straw figure, a man's scream scraped the air with an unearthly howl.

Erin shivered and watched as another man approached. He wore a gray robe, a cowled hood draped over his head. And in one hand, he held the dagger.

Turning to face the sky, the robed man stretched his arms out, imploring whatever gods he served before looking down at the earth, and lifting the dagger as Maggie had, balanced across his open palms.

The chant lifted, soaring, as the crowd of people moaned a single name. *"Abbadon."*

An icy wind kicked up, racing across the open stretch of green fields, shrieking as it passed over the people and raced on to the sea.

Erin held her breath and felt her dread build as the robed man turned to the straw figure and stabbed the dagger into the man hidden within.

Pain exploded in her head as she came out of

the vision. She staggered backward and instantly
felt Santos's arms enfold her. He pulled her close
and steadied her as she fought for balance. To find
her way back to the time where she belonged.

"I was in Ireland," she murmured. "Ancient
Ireland."

She felt him in her mind, drawing on her
memories of what she had just experienced. Erin
was grateful she didn't want to have to explain it,
relive it. As it was, she had the feeling that what
she'd seen and that hideous, moaning chant would
be a part of her dreams for a long time.

"Human sacrifice." Santos's arms banded
around her middle, holding her tightly to him as
if trying to silently reassure her that she was where
she belonged.

"Yes," Erin said with a shudder. She closed her
eyes but instantly opened them as the memory
played out for her again. "I only saw the one
violent act though, thank God. I don't know if I
could have taken many more like that one."

"The man in the robe," Santos said. "A priest?"

"Druidic, I think." Erin blew out a breath and
laid her head on his chest. Deliberately, she tried
to calm the racing pound of her own heart by listening to the steady beat of his. Still, she thought

about what she'd seen and tried to make sense of it. "But I don't understand. I thought Druids began as an earth religion. Human sacrifices? It doesn't make sense."

"In ancient times, many religions relied on a ritual sacrifice to appease their gods."

"Logically, I know that. But I've never had to watch one before," Erin muttered, remembering the screams of the man within the straw figure.

"If the dagger were used in ritual killings, it is possible that its history is well-known in some circles."

"Demon circles?" she asked, nestling in close, enjoying the sensation of having Santos holding her.

His fingers smoothed through her hair and Erin nearly sighed with the pleasure of it.

"Yes," he said and she heard the smile in his voice. "In demon circles." He paused. "Erin. The name the people chanted. It was Abbadon?"

"That's what it sounded like." She shook her head against his chest, as if the motion could somehow dislodge the voices still moaning inside her head. "Why?"

"It is the name of a powerful demon. He commands legions in his dimension."

That didn't sound good. Her heart went still as

Erin lifted her head to look up at him. "What does that mean for us?"

"I am not certain yet," he admitted, staring off into space as if already making a plan to deal with this new nugget of information. "But it is a place to start."

"Do you think it'll help your friend find us some answers?"

"I do," he said. "Rogan Butler knows much of what happens on his island."

"I hope you're right."

"You must trust me," he murmured, his voice a caress.

Outside the house, a shadow moved, slinking through the lush greenery, making itself one with the darkness. It ran one hand along the wall, testing the house's defenses, shrinking from the shimmer of wild energy that erupted at its slightest touch. A hiss of disapproval, frustration slipped from the demon as it withdrew. "Witch's barrier." It spat the words and swiped one long, narrow hand across its mouth as if it could wipe away the taste.

The demon snarled, swung into the closest tree and scrambled through the leafy branches.

Animals skittered away from it, even the tree itself seemed to shudder as a wind passed through the leaves making them chatter like frightened children.

The demon, though, clung to its branch and leaned out, looking at the house. So many lights. And people. Too many to discount. Too many to fight through to get to the one. The woman.

Time was short and the demon could not fail. The punishment for failure was too hideous to contemplate. And so it waited, alone, in the shadows, watching the house. Watching for the opportunity it needed.

Watching for the woman.

Erin leaned into Santos, relishing the feel of his rock hard body aligned along hers. *Trust.* She thought about that for a long moment or two and realized that she did trust him. More than she ever had anyone else in her life. She hadn't thought she would ever trust again after Jack Baker had betrayed her.

"If he were here," Santos said abruptly, "I would beat him for every tear he made you cry."

"What?"

"The man you cared for," Santos said, his chest

rumbling with the deep roll of his voice, "you were thinking of him and it brought you pain."

"You really need to stop peeking through my mind whenever you feel like it." Though even as she said it, she knew she'd miss the feel of his presence. Miss knowing she could reach for him with a thought and have him hear her. Miss *him.*

"Why do you still cry for him?"

"I'm not," Erin argued. "I quit crying over Jack four years ago. But when I think about it, it can still make me sad."

"Because you told him of your gift and he left you in fear?"

Shame filled her as she remembered the look on Jack's face when she showed him her abilities. She hadn't told many people in her life. Hadn't really trusted anyone since the night she'd discovered her adoptive father's guilty secret. She hadn't believed anyone would love her in spite of what she could do. After all, her own parents, the people who had *chosen* her had rejected her.

But she had been so sure that Jack was different. She'd felt happy with him. For the first time since she'd left home she'd felt safe. Comfortable. They had worked together. They had spent every free moment together. And the night he had told her he loved her, Erin had decided that she couldn't keep her secret from him any longer— not if she wanted to have an honest relationship with him.

So, she had trusted in his love. Trusted that he would see her abilities and still see *her*. The woman, not the freak.

She'd been wrong.

"He did not deserve you," Santos proclaimed. "He was a spineless fool. To be afraid of such a gift."

Erin smiled to herself at his immediate defense of her, but shook her head anyway. "He only reacted as everyone else has in my life. Everyone *says* they think psychic abilities are exciting and cool. But not so much when it's right there in your living room. People are afraid of what they don't understand. It's human nature."

"I do not fear you," Santos said, stroking his hand over her hair.

"No," she said softly, "you're different. My abilities don't worry you. I do. You don't trust me."

"What?" He tipped her head up so he could look down into her eyes. "Why do you think such a thing?"

"Because you won't let me in," she said and

lifted one hand to stroke her fingertips along his rigid jawline. "You say you love me, but you can't trust me to be a part of your life."

"It has nothing to do with trust, little one."

"I'm not that little," she pointed out, though she had to do it by tipping her head all the way back to meet his gaze, which really didn't prove her point for her. "It's all about trust. You can tell yourself you're asking me to leave because you're protecting me. Because I have no place beside a warrior. But the bottom line is, you don't trust me to be at your side."

He glared at her, but she continued speaking.

"You hold back. I feel it in you whenever we're together. There's a corner of your mind I've never breached. It's something you keep separate. Something you don't want me to see."

His features froze over. "Some things a man keeps to himself. Some things a man does not talk about, Erin."

"You could, though," she said sadly. "If you trusted me. But in your own way, you're just like Jack Baker."

"I see no reason to insult me."

She laughed shortly, in spite of the fresh wave of pain that had settled around her heart. "I'm not

trying to insult you. I'm trying to tell you I understand why you're willing to let me go. Why you
won't let yourself love me."

"You are wrong."

"No, I don't think so." She moved into his
embrace again, because she needed his touch.
Needed to feel his arms come around her. When
he held her, Erin felt safe and in her suddenly
spinning world, safety was at a premium. "I think
that sometime in your very long life, someone
betrayed you, too. And I'm the lucky girl who has
to pay for it."

He smoothed his hand up and down her spine
in what he probably thought was a calming
manner. Instead, the slide and touch of his big
hands sparked a need Erin wished she could
ignore. But it was impossible. He didn't trust her.
Wouldn't let her stay with him. Yet, Erin felt her
body's response to his and wondered if she would
ever be able to feel that way for another man.

She felt fury spike through him and then drain
away again in an instant. Clearly, he'd heard her
thoughts. Again. And just as clearly, he didn't like
her thinking about other men. Erin sighed and reluctantly stepped away from him.

"You are being unreasonable," Santos said.

"And you are being bossy, arrogant and hard-headed." She shook her head. "Too bad that's not enough to keep me from loving you."

"Erin—"

She walked to the French doors, pulled back the sheer curtains and stared out at the night. Her own reflection stared back at her, but she looked beyond the pale features etched in sadness. She fixed her gaze on the outside world where blackness awaited. Even the stars looked farther away, fainter points of light in a sea of pitch. She shivered, as if someone had walked across her grave.

Hesitantly, she touched one fingertip to the windowpane and felt an instant stab of something malevolent. Something entirely evil. Out there. In the dark. Watching her.

Erin curled her hand into a fist, sucked in air, dropped the draperies and stepped away from the window.

"What is it?"

"Something…out there…I don't know." She waved a hand at the glass and kept backing up. Erin could still feel the power of a dark gaze on her. As if it had been a cold hand reaching out to stroke her skin.

Santos was at her side in an instant, but Erin didn't dare let him touch her. If he did, she'd want to be held again, kissed again. And she'd been down that road too far already.

"What did you see?" He pulled the edge of the sheers back and stared into the night.

"I didn't see anything." Her head ached, her heart raced. "I just…felt it. Evil. Watching me."

He looked at her. "It cannot get past the barrier."

Erin nodded jerkily. She'd take that as cold comfort. The demon couldn't get to her. But she couldn't get away, either. So they were all trapped. Wasn't this a good time?

She shook her head. Rubbing her hands up and down her arms, she tried to banish the sensation of desperate cold that was invading her body. She couldn't seem to stop shivering. "I have a headache. I need some aspirin."

"Let me help you."

"No." She held up both hands as he came close. "No, I just need to be by myself." She hurried across the room, but when she reached the closed door, she put her hand on the knob and paused. "When you talk to your friend in Ireland, I want to know what he says."

Then she left him there, alone.

* * *

Santos prowled the roof of the house, stalking from one edge to the other, scanning the sky, the ground. He slipped through the shadows, becoming one with them. Unseen, wrapped in his Guardian's power of invisibility, he marched furiously, looking for a battle. Though the roof was steeply pitched, there was a widow's walk ringing the outline of the house, providing just enough room for a Guardian to walk. He had patrolled from this very spot many times since agreeing to stay temporarily in San Diego.

But never before this night had Santos so needed the satisfying clash of combat. More than anything, he needed something to fight. Needed to feel his blood pound.

But there was nothing. Whatever Erin had seen or felt was gone now, alerted, possibly, by her hand at the curtains. He lifted his face into the wind, tasted the scents, felt for trace energy signatures, but all he felt was the damp of the ocean air. Fog twisted on the horizon, pearled beneath the shimmer of the moon, and swept toward shore, like the breath of dragons.

And the Guardian, denied a battle, jumped from the battlements to rejoin the household.

* * *

By evening, the scents pouring from the kitchen were enough to bring the strongest warrior to his knees. And if the mingled aromas of spices wasn't enough, Santos thought, all he had to do was look at the chef.

Erin moved with a dancer's grace, shifting back and forth between the stove and the island counter. As he and the rest of the household waited for dinner, their private chef concentrated on food preparation.

"It smells wonderful," Amy admitted on a sigh.

"It does indeed," Thomas seconded, wincing only slightly as his wife jabbed him with her elbow.

"Are you hinting that I'm not a good cook?"

"Of course not," Thomas assured her. "It's only that, this smells…different."

"It's chicken," Erin said.

"Not like we've had before," Santos muttered.

Under the bright overhead light, Amy spared him a furious glance, too, then shrugged half-heartedly. "I'm forced to agree. When it comes to potions, I'm the best there is. When it comes to cooking…"

"It's very easy," Erin said, scraping the crushed

clove of garlic off the cutting board into the hot olive oil. "Just stir-fried chicken with garlic and a few spices over pasta." She glanced at Amy and smiled. "I can show you if you like. Nothing I enjoy more than cooking."

Santos knew that. He'd been in her mind often enough to see her love for her work, her talent for cooking. He knew she'd left behind a job she loved in New York when her world had crashed around her. He knew the joy she took from working in the kitchen and knew that right now, she needed to be busy to keep her mind off the danger surrounding her. Not to mention the heated words that had passed between them.

Yet as much as she had been shaken—as much as she'd been hurt again by their conversation in the study—she showed no sign of it now. His admiration for her blossomed. She was a strong woman, with much courage.

The garlic hissed and steam lifted off the pan. While he watched her, unable to tear his gaze away, Erin stirred the chicken, blending the spices and the oil even while her right hand reached for the pan of cooked pasta.

She tipped the contents into the pan and shook it masterfully, tossing the chicken and pasta high and catching it again over the stove's flame. When she was finally satisfied, she transferred the dish to an earthenware bowl and set it on the table.

Everyone dug in and soon, conversation flowed around the table. Santos ate, drank the cold white wine and only half listened to those he sat with. He couldn't tear his gaze from Erin. Her face was flushed, her dark red hair fell in a soft curtain along her cheeks and her emerald-green gaze was filled with questions.

Questions he couldn't answer.

Yet.

"This is amazing, Erin," Amy said.

"Wonderful," Thomas echoed.

"Is good," Nicolo allowed.

Santos ignored them all as he focused solely on Erin. He'd experienced the pain and fear that had shaken her to her core after the vision she'd endured. He'd felt her tremble in his arms and sensed her resolve to remain strong. Her life had never been an easy one, and yet she continued to smile. Continued to try. And she tugged at emotions inside him that he had thought long dead.

He would think of her always. He would remember her laugh, her sharp tongue, her passion. He would wonder where she was, if she had found love with another…even the thought of that made everything in him go cold. The image of Erin in another man's arms, sighing for him, allowing him into her body, was torture for Santos. And yet, he must endure.

She was wrong, he told himself firmly, shuttering his mind so that she couldn't read his thoughts. Of course he trusted her. This was not about trust, was it? His brow furrowed and he stabbed at the chicken on his plate. Why would he *not* trust her?

When his satellite phone rang, Santos grabbed it as he would a life line. He glanced at the screen and nodded in approval. Everyone at the table went still as he flipped the phone open and answered. "Rogan?"

Chapter 12

"Spaniard," the other man said, his voice as clear and musical as if he were in the room with them. "I've only now returned. Little bastard demon led me a merry chase all the way to Dublin and back."

Santos's gaze met Erin's and locked there, holding the two of them linked as he interrupted his old friend's storytelling. If Rogan was given half a chance, the man could talk all night. "Did you receive the message I left for you?"

"I did," Rogan said. "Interesting problem. This dagger, the hilt is black with silver inscriptions?"

"Yes. And we know more now. It was once used in a ritual sacrifice. We think Druidic."

"Ah, the lovely Druids," Rogan said. "Nasty bunch, they were. Always giving orders and such and then a few did really enjoy their bonfires and blood."

Santos felt Erin's fear climbing and in response, he sent a quick look to Nicolo and the others. Quietly, they all got up and left the kitchen, but not before Thomas snagged another piece of chicken for the road.

Erin sighed a little, braced her elbows on the table and reached for her wineglass. Taking a long sip, she nodded at him and sent him a brief, mental message. *Thanks*.

Santos nodded at her, then said, "Rogan, Erin is here with me now. I will put the phone on speaker so she can hear whatever it is you can tell us."

He punched a button, set the phone on the table between them and Erin caught herself smiling as she heard the lilt of an Irish accent coming through the phone.

"Lovely, then. Hello, Erin."

"Rogan," she said, still clutching the chilly wineglass in a hard fist, "I appreciate your help."

"Not a'tall, always happy to help a beautiful woman."

"And how do you know she is beautiful?"

"All women are beautiful, my Spanish friend."

Santos rolled his eyes and grimaced. "Rogan, I told you Erin has the sight."

"A handy trait," the other man acknowledged and one of the knots in Erin's stomach loosened. It was so very different to have her "gift" accepted as nothing out of the ordinary.

"She touched the dagger," Santos was saying. "She saw a priest sacrificing a man. And she heard people chanting the name Abbadon."

"Well, now," the man in Ireland said on a low whistle. "That changes things, doesn't it?"

"How?" Erin asked, leaning toward the phone as if she could actually see the man speaking.

"This dagger you spoke of. At the base of the blade, is there a small notch? Almost as if someone had taken a tiny bite of the steel?"

"I didn't notice," Erin admitted, looking to Santos. His frown told her he hadn't, either.

He stood up and left the room, saying only, "I will go fetch the blade to check." His long strides carried him out of the room and away from her in just seconds.

Erin knew he'd be back soon, so she leaned closer to the phone and asked, "Why does the name Abbadon change things?"

Rogan sighed and she sensed his hesitation. "Erin love…"

"This is my life, Rogan. I need to know what's happening. I need to know—"

Santos was back, faster than she would have thought possible. In his right fist was the dagger and his features were set in a thunderous expression. He sat down, laid the knife on the table between them and jabbed one finger at the small, almost unnoticeable notch at the base of the blade.

"Rogan, yes. There is a defect in the blade."

"It's no defect, Spaniard," Rogan said tightly. "It's been marked. Centuries ago, by Abbadon himself."

Erin had been reaching out to touch the knife, almost unable to help herself. But at Rogan's words, she stopped, folded her hands in her lap and laced her fingers together tightly.

Santos glanced at her, the lights in the kitchen sparking in the depths of his eyes. "Explain."

The night beyond the window looked darker than normal. It was as if every shadow in the world had banded together to make the blackest night imaginable. And that black pressed tight against the glass, as if it were a living entity, determined to reach into the light and spill its emptiness everywhere.

"There is a growing band of fools who worship Abbadon and the other higher demons," Rogan said softly. "Fifty years ago, this small band of fanatics started gathering at the sacred stones doing incantations, in general making asses of themselves. They were no bother to us or of interest to the demon realms."

"What changed?" Santos demanded.

"That dagger. Thirty years ago, it was found in an archaeological dig not far from the Burren."

"The Burren?" Erin repeated, looking at Santos for clarity.

Before he could speak, Rogan did. "It's a small rocky place in a corner of County Clare. Limestone pathways, disintegrating over time. Chunks of stone litter the ground and stand tall in other places, making up ancient tombs, cairns, ringforts and holy wells. It's a bleak spot, but filled with power, if you're open enough to it."

"Rogan," Santos demanded, his voice sharp, impatient, "what has this to do with Abbadon?"

The other man chuckled. "As impatient as ever

I see, Spaniard. Very well, then. The Acolytes, as they call themselves, stole the dagger from the dig soon after it was discovered. Used it to call up the demon himself."

Erin stiffened as a new, jagged bolt of fear leapt through her system. She made a grab for her wine-glass, took a long, deep gulp and shuddered.

Santos, in tune to what she was feeling, reached across the table, took her hand and squeezed as if to reassure her that she wasn't alone.

"Were you called in to capture the demon?" he asked.

"Aye, I was. And it was a battle to be remembered. The vicious bastard had a woman captive— tied to one of the altar stones in the Burren. The damn Acolytes were chanting and singing when I arrived, but scattered like dead leaves in a high wind as the fight began. I let them all go, as I had bigger worries on my plate at the time. Our battle took most of the night, but in the end, I had him in a net. Howling and shrieking curses and threats at me still, I shoved him through the portal."

Even now, satisfaction hummed in Rogan's voice and Erin noticed how alike the Guardians seemed to be. Warriors all, they thrived on the battles that defined their lives. They had strengths and skills that were only honed by the long centuries. Maybe it wasn't such a surprise that they could be so arrogant and sure of themselves.

"I freed the woman, took her to a hospital and left. The Acolytes had gone and without Abbadon they were no real danger—though to this day they gather, trying to call him back. So far, he hasn't obliged them. But what's any of this to do with Erin, if you don't mind my asking?"

"Someone's trying to kill me." She whispered the words, as if saying them too loudly would only bring about the threat she'd been hiding from for weeks.

"And you think it's a demon?"

"Demon and human forces alike are after her," Santos said.

Erin stared into his eyes, drawing on the courage and strength she found there. She wasn't ashamed to admit she was terrified. This new information only fed her dread.

"Thirty years ago," Santos mused, putting into words what Erin hadn't been able to. She was nearing thirty years of age. The Acolytes had summoned Abbadon thirty years ago. It couldn't be a coincidence.

"Can you find these Acolytes?" Santos asked.

"I keep watch on them at all times," Rogan said, insult clear in his tone.

"Good. Then discover what they did so long ago when they called up the demon. Find out why Abbadon came to them. What he wanted."

"Now then, Santos, I've a few demons of my own to track right here in my little corner of Ireland."

"It is important, Rogan."

A long pause, then the other man said, "Very well, then. I'll find out what I can and get back to you."

Santos punched a button on the phone, ending the connection. Still holding Erin's hand in his, he stood, then pulled her to her feet. Drawing her up close against him, his arms closed around her. Erin clung to him as the only stable point in her wildly out-of-control universe.

"You're thinking what I am," she said, her voice muffled by the solid breadth of his chest.

"Yes," he said, resting his cheek on top of her head. "There is a connection. There has to be. Abbadon visited this world thirty years ago—and now both humans and demons are after you."

She closed her eyes and willed away the tears she felt choking her. "Why is this happening?"

"We will discover the truth, Erin." His hands moved through her hair, rubbed the nape of her neck. "On this, you have my word."

"I believe you, Santos," she said, "I only hope I can live with what we find."

Santos and Nicolo stood on the roof an hour later, studying the lay of the land, waiting for any sign the demon Erin had felt earlier had returned. But there was only the sigh and surge of the ocean on the rocks below and the city lights stretching out behind the house, like brilliant jewels tossed across black velvet.

Yet there was a thick web of alarm hanging like fog over the house. No outward signs of danger presented themselves, but Santos had not survived centuries of battling the demon world without trusting his instincts.

"Something is stirring," Santos said at last, turning his back on the city to focus his sharp gaze on the trees and shrubs surrounding the estate. "I feel it in the wind."

As if conjured by his words, that icy breeze became a rush of power. Suddenly, it was as if a hurricane had touched down, blasting past them and buffeting their bodies. The scent of something powerful stained the air and only grew as the two men stood, fearless, watchful sentinels.

The wind howled like a beast in pain as Nicolo slipped the blade from his belt and held it tight in one fist.

"The safeguards will hold," Santos murmured, his eyes moving restlessly across the property.

"Against one, yes. But an army of demons?" Nicolo shrugged, as if to say it didn't matter to him if one or hundreds of demons attacked. He would stand his ground and never yield.

Santos tasted the air, still whipping past him. Ice became heat and the wind felt like a gale blown from the mouth of hell. He stared into the wind, refusing to be distracted by a show of power. The onslaught of the wind's power seemed to come from every direction at once. The heat in it tore at him and kindled his natural battle senses.

Then he noticed the sounds. A low hum of menace that built slowly into a crescendo that beat at a man's ears and hammered at his soul.

"What is that?"

Santos shook his head, unable to provide an answer. And then the first wave of insects slammed into Amy's magical barrier. They hissed and clacked and clicked as they threw themselves,

in a swarm of black, against the electrifying safeguards ringing the house. Tiny flashes of light
erupted along the tree line as the insects died in a
fruitless attack.

Santos heard the sizzle and hiss of their bodies
disintegrating as they fought for entrance. But the
safeguards held, despite the wave of shifting,
writhing black that seemed unending.

"Abbadon," Santos whispered, holding tight to
his own blade, knowing even as he prepared to
wield it that it would do little good against an
army so small and so numerous.

"He wields power over insects and can create
as many as he likes to do his bidding."

"The question then, Spaniard," Nicolo said, "is,
why does Abbadon want your woman badly
enough that he would challenge not one, but two
Guardians?"

Infuriated that he didn't have an answer for his
old friend, Santos leapt off the roof, landed in the
yard in a crouch and stalked toward the barrier that
still held against a tenacious army.

As he neared the walls though, the attack ended
as quickly as it had begun. The insects were gone
as if they had never been. All evidence disappeared and the night was quiet again. Santos

turned in a slow circle, reaching out with every sense, searching for the scent of a demon. There was nothing. Nothing for him to fight.

The night was quiet. But there was no safety in this darkness, Santos knew. Not for Erin. Not for anyone.

Not until he had found the answers he sought.

By midnight, they were in Santos's private jet, flying to his home in Barcelona. Erin walked the length of the sleek plane, her sneakers nearly swallowed by the thick, plush carpet. Bone-colored leather chairs and sofas were gathered in two separate seating areas. A desk and chair, where Santos sat at work on his computer, were tucked into an alcove. There was a small kitchen, a luxurious bathroom and even a bedroom at the back of the plane.

The hum of the engines was buzzing in her ears—like a whispered conversation she couldn't quite catch. And she couldn't seem to sit still. She kept walking, pacing, as if the constant movement would hurry them along to their destination.

She still couldn't quite believe that they'd left California behind so quickly. She'd barely had time to say goodbye to Amy and Thomas. Once

Santos had decided to leave, placing Nicolo temporarily in charge of the area, she'd had only moments to gather her things and jump into the black BMW he'd driven like a wild man to the airport. His jet was prepared and ready for takeoff when they arrived.

Now, she was on her way to Spain. A country she'd read about but had never visited. And her guide for the trip was a five-hundred-year-old stone statue of a man, lost in his own thoughts, cut off from her as neatly as if he had been on a separate plane.

Her thoughts relentlessly plagued her. Abbadon. A demon king. After her. Why? Did it want her psychic abilities? There were certainly other psychics in the world, far more powerful than she. Was it her connection to Santos that had the demon willing to chase and harass her until handing herself over to it seemed like a rational plan?

No, she told herself with a firm shake of her head. This had all started before she'd met Santos. Before she'd picked up that knife in the antique store. Before she'd turned her own life inside out in a frantic attempt to save herself.

God, she couldn't think anymore. At the galley

kitchen, she poured herself a cup of coffee and clutched it between her palms.

"Tell me again," she said. "Why are we going to Spain?"

Santos lifted his head to look at her, then closed the lid on the laptop computer for the first time since they'd left California behind. He leaned back in his oversized desk chair and studied her. His features were unreadable, his mind effectively closed to her.

"As I've told you, by going to my home, we make it that much more difficult for others to find you."

"Demons can find me anywhere," she muttered, hardly believing that she was actually saying it out loud. "You said there were portals all over the world."

"True." He stood, shoved both hands into the pockets of his black jeans and braced his long legs wide apart. "But those humans who are after you do not have the ability to use the portals. By moving you out of California, it is it harder for both human and demon to reach you. They will not find it easy to breach the security of my home."

She heard the pride in his voice and couldn't help smiling despite the curl of fear still unwinding inside her. "It's that much better than the house in San Diego?"

He snorted. "There is no comparison, *querida*. At my home, I have the advantage. I know my country better than anyone and have lived for many centuries in the home I have made impregnable."

Just hearing his voice made breathing a little easier, made the hum of the engines a little quieter and the knots in her stomach a little easier to handle. Walking to a chair, she sat, curled her legs up under her and forced herself to remain still. Taking a sip of coffee, she leaned her head against the chair back and looked up at the ancient warrior watching her with black fire in his eyes.

"Tell me about it," she said. "Spain. You were born there, yes?"

"Yes." He took the chair beside her, rested one booted foot atop his knee and smoothed his palms over the legs of his jeans. "In a small village that was near what is now Barcelona."

"When?"

"What?"

"When? What year were you born?" Erin watched his face, the soft lighting of the jet's interior throwing pale shadows over his features.

He looked at her, considered not answering and then said quietly, "It was 1460."

A jolt of something incredible hit Erin with a hard slap of reality. Even though she had known what he was, accepted that he was an Immortal and had lived through much of the history of the world, hearing that he had been born in the fifteenth century was still...flabbergasting.

He smiled, a brief twist of his full lips that told her he knew exactly what she was thinking.

She smiled in return. "You look very good for your age."

He nodded his thanks, but the smile had faded already and his eyes grew dark, full of a black heat that reached for her, drawing her in, where she most wanted to be. Where she knew she couldn't stay.

Shifting her gaze, she deliberately broke the connection and looked instead at her coffee. Questions mounted in her mind. So many, she hardly knew where to start. Ridiculous, but until this moment, she hadn't cared what he was. Where he had come from. It had been enough that he was with her. Now, though, she needed conversation. Needed to fill up the emptiness she would otherwise have wanted filled with passion.

"So when I first saw you on the ship in my vision…"

"That was the end of my first life."

"So you did die."

"Yes." He took her coffee from her, had a sip and then handed it back. "If the ocean had not claimed me, the knife wound would have." He touched the blade at his belt. The knife she had found in a store and returned to him after five long centuries.

"Then how are you here? How are you immortal, still alive after I saw you die?"

He pushed up from his chair. "At the moment of death, a man came to me, gave me a choice. To die and go forward into whatever awaited me… or to become an Immortal. To battle demons and protect humanity."

Erin tried to imagine it. Tried to "see" what had happened to him so long ago. But she couldn't. "And you decided—in a moment—to fight for eternity?"

"It was a good bargain," he said, his features giving away nothing. His eyes were dark and deep and empty of emotion as he watched her.

"Even now, so many hundreds of years later, you still believe that?"

"It was the only choice for one like me." He moved around the interior of the plane like a caged beast. Despite what he said, she felt the waves of tension rolling off of him and knew there was nothing she could do to ease him. "To fight honorably. It is all I ever wished for myself. When I was a boy, I vowed to become a fierce warrior. To fight and to serve—"

"Who?" she asked, her voice barely heard over the constant thrum of the jet engines. "Who did you serve?"

"My queen," he said, slanting her a quick glance before returning to his prowling. "Isabella of Spain."

Erin sank back into her chair as his words slammed home. He had fought for the queen who had financed Columbus's trip to America. He had been aboard— "That was one of Columbus's ships, wasn't it?" she asked as the realization sank into her. "The one you died on?"

He laughed shortly, derisively. "The *Niña*. A scow of a ship with a crew of cutthroats. Columbus himself was a pompous fool. But he had the words he needed when facing my queen. Gave her promises of glory and riches and she reached for them with both grasping hands."

"Yet you served her."

"Yes." One word, spit out as if the taste of it were bitter. "I served her. In all things. And for that—"

Erin set her coffee aside and stood up, unable to sit still while his emotions raged in the close confines of the luxury jet. She faced him, her gaze following him as he continued to stalk. "Why would a warrior have been serving on one of those ships? Why were you there?"

"Because Isabella wished it," he snapped, and now his dark eyes flashed with ancient pain, with the sharp sting of betrayal, still fresh in his mind after all those centuries. "She said she wanted me there to observe. To keep a watchful eye on Columbus and her investment in him. But the truth was, she had me sail with those brigands because her husband discovered our affair. To save her own beautiful neck, she sent me to my death."

He moved closer to Erin, each long stride pounding in her brain like a weirdly throbbing heartbeat. "For *this*, the woman I loved and trusted more than any other, betrayed me. Handed me over to the scum of the sea and waited for word of my death."

"Ricardo…" Sympathy welled up inside her

and Erin nearly choked on the need to throttle a woman long dead and buried.

"Do not feel pity for me, Erin," he said, each word gouged from his throat as if scored from gravel. "My death was long ago. My life is now. And in the years to come. My world is battle. Duty. That does not change. Isabella cannot take that from me. That she was faithless does not mean that I am." His gaze bored into hers, and the power of that stare shot through her system like a brand. "I am a warrior. Now and always."

He grabbed her, his fingers digging into her upper arms with an unleashed strength that staggered her. "I do not have room for softness in my life. I have no *need* of it."

Chapter 13

Santos felt the old, helpless rage rising up in him
again as it had that cold, stormy night so long ago.
He remembered the slide of the knife into his body
and the assassin's voice shouting, "For my queen!"

Once again, he felt the pain of betrayal, sharper
than the cut of the knife into his skin. He saw the
face of his beautiful, treacherous queen in his mind
and cursed himself for ever believing she could
love a poor man from a humble village. He had
deluded himself in life. Trusted his queen to be the
virtuous, innocent woman she had pretended to be.

He had given her all that he was, all that he

hoped to be and had vowed to defend her always. And she had repaid his devotion with betrayal. With a cold, empty death, struck down by an assassin.

His warrior's blood pounded at the insult. He hadn't even been given the opportunity to fight the man attacking him. He had died with treachery singing in his blood as the black waves rushed over his head, dragging him down into the depths of the sea.

Deliberately, he banished those memories and stared down into rich, green eyes watching him with compassion.

"I do not need your concern, little one," he said, keeping his voice soft and even, at great cost to himself. Deliberately, he let her go, releasing the tight grip he had on her arms. And as soon as he did, Santos felt adrift in a sea much emptier than the one in which he had perished so long ago.

Lifting his chin, he gathered his tremendous strength. "I live my life exactly as I wish it. As I have told you, my world is one of battles. I have no use—or need—for gentleness."

Erin shook her hair back from her face, looked up into his dark, flashing eyes and said, "You're wrong. I think you need tenderness in your life more than anyone I've ever known."

Exasperated at her infuriating stubbornness, he shoved both hands through his hair laying loose on his shoulders and ground his teeth together. "I tell you, tenderness is a trap. Love has teeth to tear a man's soul."

She ignored the clear signs of the fierce fury that held him in its grasp and reached up to cup his face between her palms. Shaking her head, she smiled into his eyes. "You're wrong again, Ricardo. But at least I understand now."

He pulled free of her touch, though every cell in his body demanded he keep her near. "You understand nothing, Erin, as there is nothing to be understood."

"It was her," Erin said, speaking despite the fact that he turned his back on her to stalk down the length of the jet again. He needed space between them or he would grab her, drag her into the plane's bedroom and bury himself inside her heat.

When he could walk no farther, he turned and stared at her. Light sifted in through the windows, bathing her in a golden sheen that danced in her hair, making it shine like a glass of the richest red wine held to a candle's flame. "What are you trying to say?"

"Isabella."

He winced at the sound of the woman's name on Erin's lips. "What of her?"

"She's the one who betrayed you. The woman who taught you to lock your heart and guard it with the same ferocity you guard the world from demons."

He snorted, though her words slapped at him. "You know nothing of me."

"I know more than you think," she said and walked toward him with slow, seductive steps. "I've been in your mind. I know your devotion to your duty. I know your pride."

"Stay back." The words ground from him like a threat. A warning he forced himself to give her lest she come too close to an Immortal on the ragged edge of control.

"She cut you to your soul," Erin said, her gaze locked with his as she moved relentlessly toward him. "She took your love and used it as a weapon to destroy you."

He labored to breathe. Straining for air even as his heart crashed in his chest. Blood pumped, his body tightened and his hands fisted at his sides.

She came ever closer, the sunlit gold dappling her body with shifting patterns of light.

"And for five hundred years, you've been caught in her trap."

"I am in no one's trap," he managed to say as she stepped within arm's reach. It wasn't true, he argued silently, stubbornly clinging to the truth as he knew it.

She shook her head and stopped, so close, he took in her subtle, floral perfume with every choking breath. She invaded him, surrounded him, filled all the empty, dark places inside him.

"Allowing her betrayal to mark you for eternity gives her more power than she deserves, Ricardo."

She lifted one hand, touched his cheek with gentle fingers, and that simple touch slipped into his soul.

Was it so simple after all? Had he allowed a long dead queen to determine the course of his eternity? Had he forgotten how to live because he had been trapped in that moment of betrayal? He scowled furiously, hating the thought that Erin might be right. Hating to have to admit that he had unknowingly given Isabella power over his life for far longer than he should have.

Erin's eyes watched him, dared him to reach

out and pull her close. Challenged him to allow the
past to die, to accept a future filled with more than
the ever-present danger that had so defined his
life.

She challenged him to not only be an Immortal…but to really *live* for the first time since
his death.

He sighed, and the breath released from his
lungs took with it the last lingering threads of a
hatred he had nursed for centuries. At last, Santos
allowed the bitterness of Isabella's treachery to
slip into the past where it belonged.

And with that decision, he felt as if he had been
freed from a cage he hadn't even been aware of
until that moment. It was as if Erin had thrown
open the bars to a prison of his own making,
allowing him to see the world…*her,* in a way he
could never have seen them before.

You humble me, he whispered into her mind.
*Your gift of love is more than I ever thought to be
blessed with.*

And you don't want me to leave?

He leaned in close, and planted a kiss as soft as
a dream on her forehead. "I will never allow you
to leave me, *querida.* Not now. Not ever."

Erin smiled at him and all the life and light in

the world was caught up in that smile. Santos reached for her, unable to bear not touching her another moment. Pulling her close, he bent his head to hers and claimed her eagerly, hungrily.

As a man in love for the first time in centuries.

A car and driver were waiting for them at the airport. They arrived at night, but even the darkness couldn't hide the beauty of Barcelona. Ancient buildings stood alongside their more modern counterparts. Lights dazzled the eyes and Erin watched the city speed past as any other tourist might. Her face pressed to the window, she strove to see it all at once.

When Santos's phone rang though, she turned to look at him, expectation warring with the fear charging through her.

He flipped it open, automatically hit the speaker phone button and said, "Rogan. You have news?"

"Aye," he said on a tired sigh. "I do. Is Erin there, as well?"

"She is." Santos reached for her and she slid across the black leather seat toward him. His arm stole around her shoulders and she leaned into his solid strength.

"Good, then I'll only have to say this once."

"Say it then and be done," Santos ordered.

"You remember I told you there was a woman tied to the altar the night I fought Abbadon some thirty years ago?" Rogan paused as if to gather his thoughts. "She was the sacrifice that night. Though she wasn't to be killed. She was to be given to the demon." Rogan paused again. "Her name was Breanna Shea."

"Bre—" Erin shot straight up. Her blood became like ice, slowing her heart. Breanna Shea was her mother. The birth mother she'd never known. The woman who had reached out from the past to deliver a warning in the hopes of keeping her daughter alive.

Santos pulled Erin close to him, holding her tightly in a vain attempt to still the shivering wracking her body.

Rogan continued softly. "Abbadon took her as his that night. She conceived and gave birth to you. She did her best to hide you, Erin. Giving you up for adoption. You see, Abbadon had told her what he planned for you. Breanna herself died in a freak accident less than a month after your birth."

Erin's mind whirled. Grief welled up for the

mother she'd never known and fear for a future that suddenly looked far more dangerous than it had even the day before.

She couldn't breathe. Couldn't stop the pulse-pounding terror coursing through her body. She lunged from Santos's arms and threw herself at the car door. Hitting a silver button, she lowered the window, desperate for air.

"What has he planned?" Santos demanded. "Tell it all, Rogan. Quickly."

"Breanna Shea, bless her, was a powerful earth witch. Her psychic powers were strong. This is why Abbadon chose her as the vessel for his child."

His child. Those two words racketed around in Erin's brain. Keeping her face near the open window, she closed her eyes and futilely tried to escape her own body. She was the daughter of a demon. The product of a sacrificial rape.

Demon blood ran in her veins.

You are no demon, Erin. Believe it.

Santos's words rushed into her mind, and she clung to them desperately. He pulled her back into the circle of his arms.

Rogan continued, "Abbadon wants Erin's life. If he kills her just before the dawn of her thirtieth birthday, the powers she inherited from her mother become his. Added to his own, it will be enough to free him from his dimension and enter ours without fear of Guardians. Then he will have the time and freedom to unleash whatever hell he chooses."

"Oh, God…" This couldn't be happening. Couldn't be real. She turned her gaze to the window and focused on the lights flashing past. Out there, people lived without fear or knowledge of demons or sacrifices. She would have given anything to be like them.

Santos turned her face to his and she stared into those dark eyes that had come to mean so much to her, half expecting to see disgust. She was half demon. He hunted demons. How could he bear to touch her?

As if to answer that question, he kissed her gently. He tucked her head into the hollow of his shoulder before asking Rogan, "What of the humans who have been trying to kill Erin *before* her birthday?"

"They are not followers of Abbadon," Rogan said, disgust evident in his tone. "They are zealots who stand opposed to the Acolytes. The dagger was stolen from the followers of Abbadon two years ago. The zealots believe the only way to keep the earth safe from Abbadon is to kill Erin before her father can take her power."

"And if she lives beyond her birthday?" Santos asked.

"Abbadon is defeated. This time, at any rate." The sound of papers rustling came through the phone and then Rogan said, "All the information I have states that the demon has wagered all on acquiring Erin the moment the stars are in alignment."

"Then all we must do is keep her safe until after the dawn of her birthday."

"All?" Erin whispered with a shake of her head. It sounded like a tremendous task to her. At the moment she felt as though every ounce of her strength had been drained away.

"My thanks, Rogan." Santos snapped the phone shut. He pulled Erin in closer. "Do not fear, *querida*. I will allow no harm to come to you."

"I'm a demon, Santos."

"No," he said firmly, clearly brooking no argument. Tipping her face up, he stared into her eyes and *willed* her to believe him. "I told you once before I sensed no evil in you. I still do not. Whatever your beginnings, you are simply Erin. My love. My life."

She closed her eyes, hugged his words to her and cuddled in closer, needing his strength, his warmth, more than she ever had before.

The luxury of Santos's Barcelona home made the mansion in San Diego look like a hunting shack. Erin wandered up and down long corridors where cream-colored walls were dotted with paintings of every type and description. There were Goyas, Picassos, Monets. Landscapes, portraits and still lifes that she had read about in books but never expected to see outside a museum.

An enormous staff moved through the halls quietly, completing their duties, yet seeming to disappear like faeries whenever she entered a room.

For days, Erin had tried to stay busy while Santos worked, hunting demons who threatened his territory, plotting ways to foil Abbadon's plans. Every night she watched him leave and every dawn she welcomed him home, into the massive bed that had become theirs.

Strange that she could be both more happy than ever before and yet still be held in the grips of a fear that was so relentless it chased her into her dreams. Daughter of a demon finds love with a

Guardian. It sounded like a bad movie plot. And yet, knowing Santos loved her was all that held the ragged threads of her sanity together.

Only two days left until her birthday and it was as if even the elements felt the nearing threat.

For days, rain pummeled the estate, beat at the windows like tiny, infuriated fists. Wind howled in off the ocean and screamed against the walls of the house. Even the air felt too thick to breathe, and the walls of the amazing house seemed to close in on Erin.

Now, as she had on previous nights, she stood on the long, flat roof of the mountaintop home, staring at the countryside spreading out to the front and sides of Santos's property. At the back of the house, the sound of the ocean had become the heartbeat of this country she was already growing to love.

In front of the house, a gray ribbon of road weaved in and out of the landscape and tiny cars maneuvered the narrow, paved highway, looking like children's toys. In the distance, craggy mountains jutted up from the earth, their jagged tips scraping the sky.

Wrapping her arms around her middle, Erin wandered the rooftop, shivering in the wind whip-

ping in off the ocean. The night sky was clear
though clouds hovered on the horizon as if gathering their strength for the next assault. Erin stared
down at the pinpoints of light, indicating lamplight
streaming through the windows of the homes below.

Santos was out there, somewhere, battling as he
had for centuries. Trying to find a way to keep her
safe. But was there a way?

She became aware then of a sudden stillness
that had settled over the area. The normal night
sounds were gone, birds and insects unnaturally
quiet. Even the pulse of the sea seemed muted.
Erin held her breath and turned slowly, toward
the ocean. Toward the threat she suddenly sensed.

Fog washed over the lip of the roof. Thick,
white, it moved as if alive, searching, reaching for
her. Fingers of damp stretched out, spreading
across the rooftop, tangling themselves around
her legs, twining ever higher, thicker around her
body. She felt as though the slender threads of fog
were chains, tightening until she couldn't draw a
breath.

Her lungs screamed for air, her mind whimpered for a place to hide. Cold delved into her
bones and a hissing voice whispered from the fog.

"Come," it said, entreating, pleading, tempting.

"Come to me and all will be well. Save yourself. Save the Guardian. Come."

Erin's mind fragmented into slivers of visions. Torn pieces of images flashed into her thoughts. *She saw her mother, lying on a stone tablet, but she wasn't chained, she was young, eager as she reached up her arms for the demon lover approaching in the moonlight. His thick, heavy body covered Breanna Shea's as a crowd chanted their approval. Their loyalty.*

"No!" She shook her head, refuting those images as the lies she knew them to be. Her mother had been a victim, not a willing participant. She had tried to protect Erin and had died too young herself.

That voice was playing with her mind. Twisting memories, images until it made her doubt herself, her own senses. She tried to close her ears to the sounds, still whispering from the fog. But it was relentless, demanding she listen. Erin wrenched herself free of the grasping fog and fought her way to the stairs that would lead her to the grounds.

But the fog kept pace, alive, impatient. She felt its presence as she would have a living, breathing enemy and Erin choked back a sob as she ran blindly down the stone stairs hugging the side of the house.

"Come to me," that insistent voice prodded her, pushed her as she ran. Slipping into her mind, her heart, it invaded her body and demanded she obey. "Run to the gate, I will save you. You need only me..."

"Santos!" She screamed his name as she bolted down the last of the stairs, her boots ringing loudly in the unearthly stillness. Her breath came in short, sharp gasps, her lungs screaming for sustenance, her mind splintering with the images sent by her enemy.

Her mother bending over an infant Erin, whispering, "Your father will come, my love. Welcome him. He is all powerful and deserves all you can give."

"She didn't say that, you bastard!" Erin's voice broke, filled with tears and shattered in the fog that had caught her in its cold, damp web again.

"Come to me!"

She knew that voice was the embodiment of the danger surrounding her. Knew that to follow that imperious command would mean her death. And yet, it was as if her own body was betraying her.

When she reached the neatly manicured lawn,

instead of racing to the house, she ran with the fog, unable to help herself, unable to stop. Though she ran toward the threat that had followed her across the world, Erin couldn't break the spell that held her.

In the thick fog, she saw...things. Creatures. Wild, red eyes and low, reptilian bodies that writhed and moaned. Terror shackled her heart, fisted her stomach and weakened her knees but still she couldn't stop. Her feet continued to move through the fog that swept higher and higher, until all around her she saw only the thick white mist that filled her lungs and closed her throat.

Taunting laughter lifted from the fog and spiraled around her in the air like ribbons of black silk.

Erin felt the pull of the voice, the overwhelming urge to obey. To fulfill its every desire. And even while she raced to her doom, she reached out with what was left of her shattered mind to Santos. The one being she knew would save her, when she couldn't save herself.

Erin! Resist. Fight.

"I can't," she said, the words torn from her throat on a sob of hopelessness.

When she reached the tall, spiked, iron gate that cut off the grounds from the road, Erin fumbled with the lock. Tugging and pulling on the heavy linked chain, she cried and screamed and wept as she opened the gate and helplessly welcomed her destroyer.

Santos felt Erin's danger. Felt the threat surrounding her. Felt the fear choking her and he hadn't been able to save her. Hadn't been able to give her the strength she needed to withstand the demon's demands.

Racing across the estate, Santos moved through the darkness like a man possessed. His sword at hand, he searched every shadow, every tree, every bush, hoping against hope that she had somehow withstood the demon.

But she was gone. And he knew it. He could sense her absence from his world like a gaping black chasm in the universe. All the light she had brought him had vanished with her.

The demon thought it had won.

"But this is only the beginning of the battle," Santos whispered and quickly scaled the wall leading to the rocky cliff and the ocean below.

He moved swiftly and doggedly, becoming a part of the night, battling the force of the wind as it smashed him against the face of the cliff. Santos wouldn't be stopped. Wouldn't surrender Erin to the demon world.

Leaping from one notch in the rocks to another, he landed on the beach moments later. Dropping into an instinctive crouch, he snarled into the dark, holding his blade high, as if in challenge. But the beach was empty of all but the incoming tide, stretching out lacey patterns on the black sand. The sliver of moon hid behind a bank of clouds and the intermittent light was enough to show Santos there were no demons at the portal.

He moved forward slowly, carefully. Every step measured. Every breath a promise of retribution. The wind plucked at his hair and tossed grains of sand into his face, his eyes. But he continued, relentless now.

Narrowing his gaze, he studied the cliff wall, finding a slash of color that marked the portal. It was closed, a mere line of pale yellow against the rocks defining the entrance to worlds unimagined by humanity. But as a Guardian, he had the power to open all portals.

Bracing his feet wide in an unconscious battle stance, Santos lifted both arms high, feeling the heavy, balanced weight of his blade. He muttered an ancient chant, the words twisting into the wind and dissolving into the pale yellow that slowly began to widen.

The portal blossomed in the darkness, glittering wildly with the weirdly pulsing light of a multitude of demon dimension. And Santos reached out with his senses, tracking, tracking as one after another hell dimension flashed past the portal, allowing glimpses into wildly different worlds. Worlds in which creatures no one could imagine thrived.

"Hold!" he shouted as he caught Erin's scent. Instantly, the spinning vortex of the portal was still, allowing a view of a deep orange sky and glittering, black onyx roads, stretching away from the portal toward a city that etched itself black against that unnatural sky.

He felt her energy. Felt her fear, choking him. She had disappeared into that dimension and was still trying to reach for him, despite the powerful demon doing its best to control her.

Her own strength was vast, yet the terror she felt at the knowledge of her bloodline clouded even her courage. And Santos's blood ran cold, as well. Normally, Guardians didn't enter the demon dimensions. They simply tossed their quarry back where they belonged. He would be stepping into unknown territory. A dimension filled with the very demons he had spent centuries hunting.

He would find no friends within.

But he had to find Erin. He couldn't allow her to be taken from him.

And he must hurry.

An Immortal could stay indefinitely within a hell dimension. But a human wouldn't last more than a few days. The atmosphere alone would kill her.

His mind reached for hers and found only a swirl of confusion, shattered thoughts. And still, Santos whispered to her.

I am coming, querida, he vowed, stepping into the portal, feeling the hot, blistering wind buffet him, trying to force him back the way he had come. Above him, the deep orange sky seemed to pulse with fury, feeding on the demons who lived below. He felt the strange charge in the air and took a breath, sneering at the taste of fire and smoke.

From a distance, shouts carried on the fiery air. Howls and screams and demonic laughter that echoed weirdly across a landscape that seemed alive with menace. Santos gripped his blade and stepped forward, into the unknown.

The portal closed behind him, snapping shut

like the jaws of a great shark over its prey. But Santos hardly heard it. His focus was entirely on the demon city before him.

And the one woman who meant life—both to himself and the demon who sought her blood.

Chapter 14

Erin's prison cell was situated high atop a castle of black stone. She still wasn't sure how she'd gotten there. The trip through the portal was a blur in her mind and the only evidence of her journey to the castle were the bruises and cuts on her body.

Dragged, she thought, smoothing her fingertips across a raw abrasion on her forearm. Blood seeped from several small cuts on her hands and legs. A knot on her forehead thumped and pounded with every beat of her heart and her throat felt as though someone had used a blow-torch on it.

Memories staggered through her mind. *A demon's face, eerie in the weird light, red eyes, slashing grin of a mouth, pointed ears and a string of a body with long fingers that dug into her arm as he pulled her along the street. Hisses rising from the crowd lining the blackened road, hanging from trees that stood, gnarled and twisted, against the orange sky. Shrieks and howls of glee staining the air, applause rising up and sounding like a stadium full of cheering fans.*

Erin held one hand to the base of her throat and stumbled across the bare cell to the only window, carved out of black stone, open to the hot, constantly moaning wind. She'd been brought to the demon dimension. To Abbadon.

She stared out the jagged opening in her prison cell at a sky the color of flames. Deep orange, the wide sky spread over a landscape she could never have dreamed of. Black trees, red trees, their leaves spiny and sharp, twisted and bent as if tortured into their shapes. Roads spilled in every direction from the castle, rising and falling in high peaks and deep gorges. Jagged. Sharp. It was as if everything here were designed to bring pain.

This wasn't Earth, she thought, fighting to draw air into her lungs. This was Abbadon's world. A

world he commanded. Here, she was the inter-
loper. A thing to be destroyed.

All around her, shrieks and wails rose up. Her
fingers clenched against the black stone and the
blistering heat trapped within singed her palms.

She clung to that physical pain as a reminder
that she still lived. That she could still think and
feel and breathe, though the air felt thick enough
to chew. It was all she had. That sense of self she
desperately clung to as the door behind her
crashed open, slamming into the wall.

Erin faced the beast who entered, its tilted eyes
as red as the flames that made up this ugly world.
"Who are you?" she asked.

"A servant," it replied, voice croaking with a
grating sound that scraped against her nerves.
"Sent to bring you before the great one."

As it grabbed her, dragging her through the door
and down a steep flight of black stairs, Erin did the
only thing she could. She called to the one man
who was her only hope of coming out of this alive.

Santos…

Santos fought like a man possessed.

He didn't bother to obfuscate himself from the
demons. Trying for invisibility now would have

been pointless since so many of the denizens of this particular hell had seen him as he stepped through the portal. He fought for every yard of ground he gained. Dipping and rolling beneath his opponents, he would spring to his feet, slash his sword through whatever was in his way and continue on.

He didn't tire, didn't waver. This is what he was born for. What he was best at. In their own dimensions, demons could be killed and he left a trail of broken, bleeding bodies behind him as he made his way to the black palace.

He felt Erin's presence. Not her thoughts—her mind was still clouded by pain and fear. And as he sensed the injuries done to her, rage exploded within him, guiding his blade, hurrying his strides.

He held the knife Erin had returned to him in his left hand and with his right, he swung his sword with deadly accuracy at every enemy who attempted to stop him. The meaty sound of steel against flesh shuddered in the air and shrieks of agony splintered around him. It only fed the fires churning within. Every dead demon was a victory. Every slice of his blade brought him that much closer to Erin.

She sighed his name into his mind and Santos's fury became the stuff of legends. He stood in the midst of his enemies, his black eyes gleaming with power, his face a mask of wrath. An ancient warrior declaring war on the demon world.

The few remaining demons challenging him scattered as Santos lifted his bloodied sword high and screamed, *"Abbadon!"*

The demon dragging Erin threw her down. She slid across the gleaming black stone floor, crashing into a dais on which another demon was seated.

"Welcome."

His voice was the sound of wheels spinning in gravel and it seemed to echo over and over again in the vast chamber.

Tall, the demon had brick-red skin, glittering onyx eyes and a victorious grin that gave Erin chills.

"I am Abbadon," he said, lifting both hands wide as he watched her. "Your father."

Erin swallowed hard, scooted back on the floor and pushed herself to her feet. She had to lock her knees to keep from collapsing, but she managed. She wouldn't show him the fear nearly choking her. Wouldn't let him see the desperation pounding inside her.

Her father.

She had come from *this*.

The demon prowled the edge of the dais, never taking his empty gaze from her. His footsteps were loud clacks of temper. "You have caused me much trouble."

"Really?" She swallowed hard and glanced warily at her surroundings. They were alone, though even the high, black walls of the room seemed alive with venom. Long, deadly looking stalactites hung from the ceiling. They, too, were black and glistened as they shifted and twisted in an unseen wind.

She stared hard at them, nearly hypnotized by their slow, undulating sway. Then she realized they weren't made of stone, but of hundreds, thousands, of insects, each alive and bristling with menace as they clung to each other in ever distorting shapes.

Erin muffled the groan threatening to escape her and hunched her shoulders as if that action alone would prevent the bugs from dropping down on top of her.

"Have you no thanks for me, your father?" Abbadon demanded.

"Thanks?" she whispered, her throat still raw, her heart still choking her. "You want thanks for trying to kill me? For dragging me away from my home? My world?"

He set his clawed fingers at his hips and shook his elongated head. "I have saved you from those who would have prevented you from fulfilling your destiny."

"Which is?" she asked, though she knew. She knew all too well.

"To give me the power I need to conquer your world. To rule as I always should have done," he snapped, irritation fueling his steps, each one a little shorter, harder, louder, more furious. "I command thirty legions in this dimension. I rule the abyss whose opening will signal the end of days." He whirled around, pinned her with those black eyes and said, "And on the dawn of your birth plus thirty human years, I will claim the power. I will taste victory at last and bring my legions through the abyss."

"I won't let you," she said, and didn't know how he heard her, since it sounded to her as if her voice was lost in the thundering beat of her heart.

He laughed and the sound rolled off the walls, making the insect stalactites tremble, and settled in the pit of Erin's stomach like a hot stone.

"You are much like your mother. She, too, attempted to fight me. She was a powerful psychic. A witch of strength. I knew she would provide me with the vessel I required." He sneered at the memory of the woman he'd used and discarded so long ago. Then, reaching to his own neck, he pulled a medallion and chain free and tossed it to her.

Instinctively, Erin caught it. Her mother's face smiled at her, caught forever in the energy traces clinging to the medallion. Breanna Shea had worn this silver Celtic cross every day of her life. It had been handed down from daughter to daughter in her family.

Generations of Shea witches had worn the cross with pride. With faith. With power.

Erin sensed her mother's magic and felt a wave of love for the woman who had suffered so much, yet still had fought to save the child she had had to give away.

Deliberately, she stopped the flood of memories seeping into her soul. Later, later, she would cling to it like a talisman and try to draw on the strength of the family she had never known.

"I kept it," Abbadon said, his voice dropping another octave, into a range that thrummed like the rumble of a powerful engine. "Her essence was caught there and you were a part of it. I traced you through that piece of foolery. And now, it comes full circle."

Other memories crowded in, despite her attempts to stave them off. Terrifying, vicious. The night as Abbadon's captive. Erin felt her mother's strangling fear and her determination to survive.

Erin's fingers closed around the aged, hand-worked silver that felt warm with the generations of power enshrouding it. She felt her mother's strength fill her and Erin blessed Breanna for that one last gift. Staring up into her father's empty eyes, she drew on the energy in the necklace by generations of her family's women. "I will find a way to stop you."

He dropped to one knee, peered into her eyes and smiling that hideous smile, he said, "You cannot stop me. By this time tomorrow, your world will lie in ruins and I will be its king."

Erin gasped. "It's two days to my birthday—not tomorrow."

"Ah, time moves a bit more quickly here, my child," he said. "Tomorrow, the new world begins."

Invisible now, Santos moved through the alien landscape, squinting into the fiery sun and the blistering wind. He avoided the clumps of demons gathering at the foot of the mountain and following Erin's scent, he began to climb. Trails, handholds and notches were etched into the black stone, but the rock itself felt as if lava were flowing behind it. It radiated heat, shimmering into the air, burning all those who would risk the climb.

Santos wouldn't be stopped. Continually, he reached for Erin, his thoughts winging to her. *I am near,* querida.

He heard only silence, and it filled him with more dread than facing a thousand demons.

His enormous strength carried him up the mountain to the foot of the castle walls. More black stone, glistening in the ever-wavering, fiery light. Here, there were no handholds. No way to climb the slick, smooth stone. He would have to go in through the wide gate, past the demon hordes who milled about in anticipation of the ritual.

Still using the power of his thoughts, he kept himself invisible to all as he moved stealthily through the crowd. Snatches of laughter, shrieks of pain, whispers of threats and fury rose and fell around him like waves on a never-ending sea. One after the other, the voices assaulted him, but Santos was immune. He closed his mind to all but thoughts of Erin.

Santos no longer reached out for her. He couldn't risk the demons also picking up on his presence. Instead he relied on his Guardian powers. He narrowed his gaze and instantly was swamped with the dizzying patterns of trace energy that swirled around the demon world like human auras. He studied them all as his steps continually took him higher and higher still into the mouth of the castle.

At the top of the stairs, he stopped, scanning the long, narrow dark hallway with every one of his senses. He searched through the wash of demonic color, looking for one trace energy signal different from the rest. And at long last he found it. A pale smear of the lightest blue clung to a door on the right side of the hall. Santos sprinted toward it, uncaring now if anyone heard him moving. All that mattered was Erin.

The door wasn't locked because the demons knew she had nowhere to go. What would have been the need or the point of imprisoning her? He threw the door open, stepped inside and instantly felt a smashing blow to his jaw.

"Santos!" She whispered the word and threw herself into his arms.

His sword and knife clattered to the stone floor so that he could hold her as tightly as he needed. Santos buried his face in the curve of her neck and smiled, despite the situation. Despite the danger bristling all around them. "Your first thought was to hit me, little one?"

Her voice came muffled against his chest and broken by the sobs wracking her small form. "I thought you were a demon, coming to take me away again. I thought—I had to do something…"

His chest swelled with pride. Though she was a prisoner, she didn't admit defeat. She would fight to the last. He could do no less.

"You did well," he said.

"I didn't hear you calling me and I—"

"I could not risk a mental link inside the castle," he explained, pulling her back so that he could look into her eyes and assure himself that she was indeed alive.

Her eyes shimmered with tears she refused to shed. There were scrapes and bruises on her arms and a deep, violet bruise on her right cheek. He cupped the abused spot with his palm and hissed in a breath. "For this alone, Abbadon dies."

Erin covered his hand with hers, desperate to feel the raw, incredible strength of him, here with her. "I knew you'd come."

"For you, *querida*," he whispered, "I will always come for you, no matter the cost, no matter the distance." He drew her close and took her mouth in a plundering, desperate assault.

She clung to him, feeling the power shifting beneath his muscled back, knowing that he was here for her and would find a way to save them both. When they finally tore apart, each of them breathless, Erin laid both hands on his chest and looked into his beloved eyes.

"My…father says the ritual is set for the morning."

He nodded, clearly unsurprised at the difference in time in the demon dimension. "There will be no ritual. This I swear. If we can keep you alive until dawn, whatever Abbadon is planning will fail."

"He told me," she said, stepping back and wrapping her arms around her middle. "He's going to use the power he takes from me to open some abyss so that he can loose his demons on our world."

"He will not." His voice dropped to a low throb of ferocity. "He will die before dawn."

She looked at her Guardian, standing there in

the tiny cell where she'd already spent too many desperate hours and she believed in her soul that nothing could stop this man. He looked wild, ancient, powerful. His dark hair hung loose around his shoulders, his black eyes flashed with a fury she'd never seen before and his body seemed to ripple with repressed strength, as if he were holding himself in on a very tight leash.

A sense of safety filled her, easing the terrible crush of fear and dread that had been choking her since coming through the portal. With Santos at her side, Erin felt as though she could do anything.

Santos felt the waves of trust and faith coming from Erin and he was more touched than he had ever been. And also more uneasy. He loved her with his every breath, he could admit that now and be glad of it. But he knew that to free Erin, they had to not only escape the demon stronghold, but kill Abbadon. Even if her father's plans were destroyed, the demon would never allow Erin to survive.

She would never be safe as long as the demon lived.

He cast one glance at the jagged window opening and noticed that the deep orange sky had already lightened to a watery shade. The demon dawn was not far away. Grabbing his sword and knife from the stone floor, he thrust the bone-handled knife at Erin and said, "I must find Abbadon before the ritual begins. Keep this with you. Use it on anyone who enters this room."

She shook her head as her fingers closed around the hilt of the blade until her knuckles whitened. "Take me with you."

"No." It tore at him to leave her here, but taking her into his battle with the demon was far more dangerous. "I will take care of the demon, then return for you."

"We can't escape. They'll never let us go."

"I will protect you," he promised her, cupping the back of her hand in his palm and drawing her close for a kiss. "Trust me, *querida*," he whispered, then left as quietly as a thought.

He followed his senses, reaching out through the horde of demons gathered below to find the one beast he sought among the many. Down jagged corridors lined with burning torches jutting out from the black walls, Santos moved with the stealth of a born hunter. No wasted motions. No hesitation. He sought his quarry and would not stop until he was successful.

His mind rebelled as a powerful force struck out at him, drawing him in even as it sneered at him. Santos reacted instantly, following the source of that black stain of might to a wide door at the end of a hall.

He entered, closed the door behind him and stood, ready for whatever challenge came to him. He drew on his centuries of life. Of battle. Of courage. His vow to protect humanity…Erin…swelled within him, and his terrible power shook the very air.

"Guardian."

A low hiss of sound drew Santos's eye to the far corner of the darkened room. Flames burned high on the walls, torches tossing twisted shadows and light onto the black-as-pitch stone. "You would dare challenge me in my world?"

"Demon, you are the one who issues the challenge. Who threatens a woman under my protection. A world I have vowed to defend."

Abbadon stepped from the shadows, his long, lean, red body highlighted by the firelight flashing weirdly in the gloom. His hands were curved into claws, whipping at the air as if testing his own strength for the coming fight. "The woman is mine. My daughter. I created her for this very purpose and you will not stand in my way."

"Yet, I am here," Santos said, moving into the room, slashing the air with the blade of his sword until the steel sang a low moan of warning.

"Let it begin then." Abbadon rushed him with a snarling yowl of fury. Slashing with its claws, the demon drew first blood, dragging a talon across Santos's chest.

He barely felt it. Adrenaline pumped through his system, giving his already incredible strength a burst of power that had him dipping beneath the demon to deliver a stabbing blow.

Abbadon whirled out of reach, snapped its jaws in rage and came at him again. Low and swift, the demon dipped and swayed, making an impossible target. But Santos had been a warrior for centuries. Had fought more demons than made up Abbadon's legions. And he had yet to lose a fight.

Leaping up and over the demon, Santos landed on the balls of his feet and spun in a sharp, tight arc, swinging the sword again with deadly accuracy. Abbadon shifted at the last moment and felt only the wind of the blow pass over him.

On and on they fought, the demon's snarls and hisses becoming a part of the air in the room. Minutes? Hours? Time held no meaning. Only the fight.

The blistering, searing heat wore on Santos and he used every ounce of his strength to remain strong in the most important battle he would ever fight. Again and again, he tore chunks from the demon, inflicting hundreds of small cuts and stabs. Dark blood ran down the demon's body but still Abbadon kept fighting.

Crouching low, the demon spat at the Guardian and swung one long, scaled leg out in an attempt to knock Santos off his feet.

Santos, though, was prepared for treachery. When fighting demons, the first thing a Guardian learned was to always expect the unexpected. He stabbed the tip of his blade into the demon's thigh and gave a grim, satisfied smile at Abbadon's howl of pain.

The demon then turned and bolted for the far end of the room with Santos right behind him. Abbadon leaped up onto the wall, grabbed a sword from where it hung and landed in a crouch, holding the blade at the ready.

Santos laughed. "You think to fight me with a sword? Fool. I have battled more of your kind with a blade in my hand than you could ever hope to know."

"Show me then, Guardian. Take me now or die so that I may destroy the woman you protect."

The sheer glee in the demon's hissing voice warned Santos that time was running out. He threw one quick glance out a firelit window at the sky beyond. The sweep of orange was paler now, soft, pastel, as if readying for the appearance of the brilliant, white sun.

Dawn. Only a few more moments until dawn. Until she was safe.

"You're wrong, Guardian," Abbadon said, moving in for a strike. The tip of his blade jabbed at Santos's shoulder and blood welled up. "You cannot reach her in time."

The demon laughed and the sound pierced Santos's head like a spike driven in by Thor himself.

"This is *my* world. I am not bound by human rules. By your pitiful powers and strength. I can reach her in a blink. I can reach her *anywhere.* You have not saved her. You have only entertained *me.*"

Erin... For the first time in his too-long life, Santos knew real fear. If Abbadon shifted to Erin, there would be nothing he could do to save her. The only hope then was in striking a fatal blow before the demon could move.

As if reading his mind, the demon struck first.

Abbadon's sword sliced into his upper right arm and Santos's sword fell from nerveless fingers.

The door behind them swung open with a crash and both demon and Guardian stared at Erin, striding into the room. Santos's blade clutched in one fist, she faced them both. "I heard," she said. "Heard it all."

She had linked with him during the fight. Santos should have felt that connection but his force and strength of will had been completely focused on his demon foe.

"Stay behind me," Santos ordered, shifting his gaze back to Abbadon, bending to pick up his blade, willing his fingers to heal, to grasp the steel and end this once and for all.

"No!"

Stunned, Santos hesitated. He watched Abbadon's eyes widen in rage and helplessness. And his heart sinking, Santos turned to see what the demon was watching.

Erin pointed the tip of Santos's knife, the one he had given her, at her breast. Her gaze, filled with love, met his for one long moment, then shifted to the demon who was her beginning. It was to Abbadon she spoke.

"I won't allow you to use me. To take my power and use it to destroy anything ever again. I won't allow you to injure Santos further." She inhaled sharply, lifted her chin and speared her father with a look. "I won't allow you to win."

"Erin, *no!*" Santos read her thoughts, felt her determination and the ugly decision she had reached for *his* sake. For the sake of the world.

She smiled, glanced at the sky outside, then shoved the blade deep into her own chest. Her sigh of pain was swallowed by Abbadon's bellow of pure, undiluted rage.

In his overwhelming grief, Santos still did his duty. As the first fingers of dawn stole across the sky, he lifted his sword, swung his arms back and brought the blade around in a powerful arch. The demon king's head fell from his body and rolled into the shadows.

Broken, battered, bleeding, Santos ran to Erin, dropped his sword and gathered her into his arms. His own knife, the one he had given her for protection, jutted up obscenely from her breast and her life's blood streamed from the wound. One look told him there was nothing he could do. The woman he would have given his life for was dying and there was no way to save her.

"*Querida*, why? Why would you do this?" He smoothed her hair back from her face and felt his own heart shatter into a million jagged pieces.

She smiled and slowly lifted one hand as if to touch him. She was so weak though, he caught her hand and held it to his cheek.

"It was the only way," she said, her voice no more than a breath. One of the few she had left. "You could not have gotten me out of here, Ricardo. The demons would have killed you."

"No," he said, bending, kissing her forehead, her eyes, her lips.

"My father's dead. And you live. That's all that matters."

"*Querida…*" How could he live with an aching, empty hole inside him? How could he face centuries without this woman at his side? How could he ever survive the withering pain crumpling him in its cold fist?

"I love you," she said on her last breath. Her body went limp in his arms and Santos cradled her close. Rocking her quietly in the shifting, firelit shadows, he felt more alone now than he ever had before in his life. She was everything. She was the air he breathed. The earth he trod. The water he drank. Without her…

* * *

Erin came back with a gasping breath that rattled through her lungs and sent sharp, slashing pains throughout her body. Blinking wildly, she looked at the knife in her chest, and then up, into Santos's tear-filled, awestruck eyes.

"*Querida!* You live."

"How?" She winced, moaned and pulled at the blade embedded in her chest. In a swift motion, Santos pulled it free and she nearly shrieked at the pain. "What is going on? I died. I remember dying. I told you I loved you and then I died. So why am I alive? Why am I in pain? And what the hell happened to my big sacrificial exit line?"

Laughing, crying, Santos held her close. He kissed her face, her mouth, tasted her tears and gave her his. He felt her heart pounding in a frantic, erratic rhythm and blessed every beat.

"Santos, what the *hell* is happening?" She pushed out of his arms, tore her dark green blouse open and stared in wonder at her unmarked, completely healed chest. The only reminders of what she had done were the streaks of blood, still so fresh they had yet to dry.

Santos's mind raced. His joy was unbounded, his confusion just as rich and deep, but he had an idea of what had happened. "We will find the answers at home, *querida,* though I suspect the truth."

"What?" Erin threw her hair back from her face and grabbed fists full of his shirt. "Tell me."

He shook his head, cupped her beloved face between his palms and stared directly into her deep green eyes. "Your father wanted to kill you before dawn."

"Yes."

"Yet, *you* killed yourself, just as dawn began."

"I remember that." She let go of him with one hand and rubbed the spot on her chest where she had shoved that knife.

"You must have come into your power at dawn."

"Then why would he want to kill me before dawn?"

"Not your psychic power, Erin," he said softly, his fingers tracing the line of her jaw, her throat. "Your immortality."

"Huh?"

Delighted with her exasperation, he laughed like a madman, grabbed her close and hugged her so tightly, he thought he might never let her go. "Your father is a demon. Immortal. Clearly, *querida,* you inherited this gift from him."

"Immortal?" she asked, wriggling free to stare up at him in the weird, dancing light. "Are you sure?"

"It is the only answer," he said, standing now and reaching down one hand to pull her to her feet. "If Abbadon killed you before dawn, he would receive your psychic gifts and you would have remained dead. At the dawn, you became immortal and his plan would have failed."

"Immortal," she repeated, watching him as he bent to pick up his knife and his sword, returning them to the sheaths at his belt. "Like you."

"Like me," he said, smiling and leaning close to plant another kiss on her forehead. He couldn't kiss her enough. Couldn't touch her enough. He had come so close to losing her forever, Santos didn't think he would ever be able to bear being away from her.

"Never endanger yourself like that again, Erin. Never. Even with immortality, I could not go through seeing you in pain again."

"It was the only way I could think of to thwart Abbadon and save you," she said, throwing her arms around his neck, leaning into him. "You never would have been able to get me through all of the demons standing between us and the portal. But by yourself, you could be invisible. Safe."

Santos groaned and lifted her off her feet. Swinging her up into his arms, he frowned at her. "You should have trusted me, *querida*. With the power of the connection we share, you can share the disguising shield with me. You, too, will be invisible to the demon world."

"I—" Her mouth snapped shut as she linked her arms around his neck. "You might have mentioned that."

Still holding her close, he headed out of the empty room where Abbadon lay as dead as his dreams of glory. Taking the stairs, he wove the obfuscation cloak around them, shielding them both from being seen or heard by the demons as he headed for the portal and home.

"You are a most stubborn woman," he said, but couldn't keep a proud smile from his face. "And a woman of great courage."

"I'm really tired, too. I think we should go to bed for a week."

"You will find no rest in our bed, *querida*," he promised.

"Good." She nestled her head against his chest and sighed. "Is your life always this exciting, Ricardo?"

His arms tightened around her, his strides

lengthened in his haste to get her back to Barcelona. Back to his home, where she belonged.

"*Querida,*" he said, grinning now as the centuries ahead of them stretched out with the promise of more joy than any Immortal had a right to, "*nothing* in my life is as exciting as *you.*"

* * * * *

Can this man of duty risk his heart?

Keegan McKettrick has learned the hard way that
women can't be trusted. And then beautiful but
mysterious Molly Shields arrives on a mission…

Molly doesn't know why she's attracted to a man
who's determined to dig up dirt on her,
even if he *is* gorgeous.

But cynical Keegan might be the one person
who can truly understand her shadowy past…

Available 16th January 2009

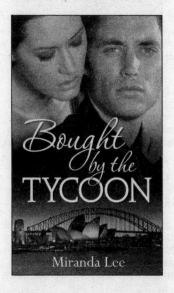

4 FREE

BOOKS AND A SURPRISE GIFT!

We would like to take this opportunity to thank you for reading this Mills & Boon® book by offering you the chance to take FOUR more specially selected titles from the Intrigue series absolutely FREE! We're also making this offer to introduce you to the benefits of the Mills & Boon® Book Club™—

- ★ FREE home delivery
- ★ FREE gifts and competitions
- ★ FREE monthly Newsletter
- ★ Exclusive Mills & Boon Book Club offers
- ★ Books available before they're in the shops

Accepting these FREE books and gift places you under no obligation to buy, you may cancel at any time, even after receiving your free shipment. Simply complete your details below and return the entire page to the address below. You don't even need a stamp!

YES! Please send me 4 free Intrigue books and a surprise gift. I understand that unless you hear from me, I will receive 6 superb new titles every month for just £3.15 each, postage and packing free. I am under no obligation to purchase any books and may cancel my subscription at any time. The free books and gift will be mine to keep in any case.

19ZED

Ms/Mrs/Miss/Mr ....Initials ....

BLOCK CAPITALS PLEASE

Surname ....

Address ....

....

...................................Postcode...................................

Send this whole page to:
UK: FREEPOST CN81, Croydon, CR9 3WZ